FIRSTS, LASTS & ONLYS

MILITARY

First published in the United Kingdom in 2007 by
Robson Books
10 Southcombe Street
London
W14 0RA

An imprint of Anova Books Company Ltd

ISBN 9781905798063

A CIP catalogue record for this book is available from the British Library.

10 9 8 7 6 5 4 3 2 1

Printed and bound in Great Britain by Cromwell Press Ltd, Trowbridge, Wiltshire.

This book can be ordered direct from the publisher.
Contact the marketing department, but try your bookshop first.

www.anovabooks.com

FIRSTS, LASTS
& ONLYS

MILITARY

JEREMY BEADLE
& IAN HARRISON

**ROBSON
BOOKS**

CONTENTS

First friendly fire fatalities of the Second World War 1939
First RAF fatality of the Second World War 1939
First British aircraft to shoot down an enemy aircraft in the Second World War 1939
First British capital ship lost in the Second World War 1939
First RAF air raid of the Second World War 1939
First British civilian fatalities from direct military action in the Second World War 1940
First British parachute raid 1941
First German submarine captured by the British in the Second World War 1941
First RAF prisoner of war to make the 'home run' from Germany 1941
First operation by the SAS 1941
First prisoner of war captured by Americans in the Second World War 1941
First US Forces arrive in Australia 1941
First air raid on Australia 1942
First Japanese attack on US mainland 1942
First US warships named after more than one person 1942
First major naval battle in which neither side sighted the other 1942
First land victory of the Second World War over the Japanese 1942
First US Soldier's Medal awarded to a woman 1943
First V1 attack on England 1944
First jet fighter to engage an enemy in combat 1944
First jet fighter to be shot down 1944
First atomic bomb used on an enemy 1945
First conscientious objector to be awarded the Medal of Honor 1945
First Nazi war criminal to be hanged at Nuremberg 1946
First coining of the term 'Cold War' 1947
First country to constitutionally abolish its army 1948
First jet-to-jet aerial victory 1950
First sinking of a large warship by a surface-to-surface guided missile 1967

❊ Lasts

Last Viking invasion of England 1066
Last successful invasion of England 1066
Last act of mercy by Richard the Lionheart 1199
Last English king killed on a battlefield 1485
Last charge of mounted knights 1485
Last Scottish king to offer battle in England1513
Last Scottish king to die in battle 1513
Last major naval battle solely between rowing vessels 1571
Last words of King Gustavus Adolphus 1632
Last pitched battle on English soil 1685
Last British king to personally lead troops into battle 1743
Last battle on English soil 1745
Last pitched battle on mainland British soil 1746
Last invasion of the British mainland 1797
Last words of Lord Nelson 1805
Last journey of Lord Nelson 1805
Last naval fleet action under sail 1827
Last use by the British Royal Navy of the word 'larboard' 1844
Last British brigade cavalry charge 1854
Last words of General John Sedgwick 1864
Last words of the Duke of Valencia 1868
Last of the Samurai 1877
Last time British infantry wore scarlet tunics in battle 1885
Last surviving veteran of the War of 1812 1905

Last US Civil War veteran to die as a result of wounds from the war 1914
Last words of Saki 1916
Last soldier killed in the First World War 1918
Last occasion a British army unit used scaling ladders 1919
Last British soldier executed by firing squad 1920
Last Royal Navy left-handed salute 1923
Last lance in the British army 1927
Last survivor of the Charge of the Light Brigade 1927
Last RAF bombing raid without a fighter escort 1939
Last BEF evacuee to leave Dunkirk 1940
Last successful invasion of the British Isles 1940
Last exchange of fire with enemy combatants on mainland British soil 1940
Last day of the Bataan Death March 1942
Last American soldier shot for desertion 1945
Last V2 rocket of the Second World War 1945
Last British civilian casualty of the Second World War 1945
Last bomb on London in the Second World War 1945
Last public appearance of Adolf Hitler 1945
Last newsreel produced by Joseph Goebbels 1945
Last words of all ten Nazi war criminals to be hanged at Nuremberg 1946
Last survivor of the Battle of Little Big Horn 1950
Last day of the First World War 1958
Last grog ration 1970
Last US soldier killed in combat in the Vietnam War 1973
Last US Army horse 1976
Last military invasion of British sovereign soil 1982
Last battle on British sovereign soil 1982
Last surviving VC-winner of the First World War 1988
Last survivor of the Boer War 1993
Last survivor of the ANZACs who landed on the first day at Gallipoli 1997

❏ Onlys
Only military campaign settled by a game of chess 1078
Only besieged army entirely saved by women 1140
Only blind commander never to lose a battle 1424
Only commander to become a drum 1424
Only country whose entire military consists of foreign-born soldiers 1506
Only fatalities ever suffered by the Papal Swiss Guard 1527
Only battle in which both leaders were captured by the enemy 1562
Only war started with three men thrown into a pile of manure 1618
Only military leader killed with his own wooden leg 1649
Only war fought over an ear 1739
Only British soldiers allowed to wear their swords in the mess 1746
Only British admiral executed for neglect of duty 1757
Only sea battle won by cavalry 1795
Only meeting of Nelson and the Duke of Wellington 1805
Only army created as a result of a fly swat 1831
Only army to enlist recruits with assumed identities 1831
Only war the British fought for drugs 1839
Only regiment massacred three times 1840
Only recipient of the VC to have held every rank from private to Major General 1858
Only war caused by a pig 1859

Only person present at the first and last moments of the American Civil War 1861
Only military order to regard hostile women as prostitutes 1862
Only fighting regiment deliberately composed entirely of old men 1862
Only draft-dodging US president 1863
Only bereavement letter sent by Abraham Lincoln to a mother who lost five sons 1864
Only VC won for action in Canada 1866
Only survivor of Custer's last stand 1876
Only combat animal decorated by a reigning monarch 1881
Only travel agency to organise transport to take an army to war 1885
Only war to last thirty-eight minutes 1896
Only British prime minister to have escaped from a prisoner of war camp 1899
Only army saved by a fleet of taxi cabs 1914
Only man to win the Victoria Cross and an Olympic gold medal 1914
Only two-man army to take on a nation 1915
Only act of international aggression to take place on Australian soil against Australian people 1915
Only British woman to have officially fought in the First World War 1915
Only dead soldier to become a national leader 1916
Only airman to fall out of a plane and fall back in 1918
Only British soldier to win five top gallantry medals without firing a shot 1918
Only English soldier who had the chance but didn't kill Hitler 1918
Only soldier to spend the whole of the First World War in a cupboard 1918
Only dog officially enlisted in the ranks of the Royal Navy 1939
Only world war started by a hoax 1939
Only person to volunteer to be imprisoned at Auschwitz 1940
Only Luftwaffe prisoner of war to escape and make it back to Germany 1941
Only animal to have been an official Japanese prisoner of war in the Second World War 1942
Only British soldiers executed for mutiny during the Second World War 1942
Only sex symbol to invent a military weapon 1942
Only US sea battle in which five brothers lost their lives 1942
Only US soldier to win the Bronze Star and the Purple Heart at the age of twelve 1942
Only attempt to use bats as bombs 1943
Only VC awarded solely on evidence given by the enemy 1943
Only animal awarded the Distinguished Service Cross 1943
Only military plan successfully undertaken by a man who never was 1944
Only Allied jet aircraft to see active service in the Second World War 1944
Only member of the British Army to receive the Military Medal three times in the Second World War 1944
Only US president to have been shot down as a military pilot 1944
Only Second World War soldier to capture an entire village on his own 1944
Only British queen to have volunteered for military service 1945
Only fighter pilot imprisoned and decorated by his country for the same act 1945
Only US mainland fatalities in the Second World War 1945
Only American deserter executed in the Second World War 1945
Only British general buried at Arlington Cemetery 1950
Only cat to be awarded the Animal VC 1950
Only court martial for peeling potatoes improperly 1959
Only Green Beret to achieve a No 1 record on the US Billboard chart 1966
Only US naval ship to surrender in peacetime without a fight 1968
Only war lasting over three centuries 1986
Only surrender induced by rock 'n' roll 1990
Only war predicted by pizzas 1991

☆ FIRST recorded intelligence-gathering operation

Canaan. c.1250BC

The first record of intelligence gathering appears in the book of Jewish scriptures known as the Torah. In chapter 13 of the book Bamidhar ('In the Desert'), aka The Book of Numbers, God instructs Moses: 'Send men to scout the land of Canaan, which I am giving to the Israelite people.' Each of the twelve tribes supplied one spy each who spent forty days recce-ing the land. They returned with disappointing news. Historians give the date of the Exodus at around 1250BC, or the year 2449 according to the Jewish calendar.

☆ FIRST precisely dated battle

Mesopotamia (now Iraq). Wednesday 28 May 585BC

This battle between the Lydians and the Medes can be precisely dated by astronomers because records state that at the height of the fighting both armies laid down their arms in terror when the sun was blotted out by a total solar eclipse.

☆ FIRST 'last stand' of note

Battle of Thermopylae, Laconia, Greece. Greco-Persian Wars. Wednesday 19 September 480BC

The warrior-nation of Spartans believed that one day either Sparta would be conquered and left in ruins or that one of her kings must sacrifice his life to defend her. In 480BC, an alliance of Greek city-states led by the Spartan king Leonidas fought Persian invaders commanded by King Xerxes. Knowing he would be vastly outnumbered Leonidas considered it a suicide mission, and when his wife asked what she should do Leonidas replied: 'Marry a good man, and have good children.' The only way to prevent the invasion was for the Greeks to defend a narrow mountain pass named Thermopylae (meaning 'hot gate', referring to a nearby sulphurous spring). Xerxes expected the Greeks to capitulate but when he sent a messenger demanding the Greeks surrender Leonidas famously answered: 'Come and get us.' Greek morale was so high that when a Spartan soldier was told that Persian arrows would be so numerous as to blot out the sun he shouted, 'So much the better, we shall fight in the shade.' The first wave of 10,000 Persians was 'cut to pieces' at the cost of only two or three Spartan lives. On the second day Xerxes sent in the Immortals, an elite corps of 10,000 men (sometimes reported as 20,000). They too failed, despite being lashed by their officers to prevent them withdrawing, their morale broken by having to climb over the corpses of fallen comrades. But then a traitor sealed the fate of the Greeks. A local named Ephialtes betrayed them by revealing a mountain path that led behind the Greek lines, and guiding the Persian army through the pass – Ephialtes is now synonymous with 'traitor' in Greek. Realising the situation Leonidas decided on a last stand, dismissing his army except for 300 Spartans with sons old enough to take over the family responsibilities, who pledged to fight to the death, and 700 Thespians who volunteered to fight beside them. The Persians eventually surrounded the remaining Greeks after sustaining enormous losses and finally Xerxes ordered a shower of arrows – a tactic the Spartans considered cowardly – to rain down until the last man was killed. But it was a pyrrhic victory because the heroism of this Spartan-led last stand ultimately led to Persian defeat and the end of the expansion of the Persian Empire into Europe. John Ruskin described the epitaph on the Spartan burial mound at Thermopylae as the noblest sentiment expressed by man: 'Stranger, go tell the Spartans, that here we are buried, obedient to their orders'.

DID YOU KNOW?

Today Spartan (*previous entry*) means austere, or lacking luxury, and refers to the original inhabitants of Sparta, the capital of Laconia, Greece, who were indifferent to common comforts. The Spartans believed they were direct descendants of Hercules. All babies were inspected by the elders who ordered that the weak or those with defects be abandoned and left to die. At the age of seven, survivors left home and learned discipline through gymnastics, dancing and ball games. At twelve they had to run a gauntlet of older children who would flog them with whips, and mothers presented their sons with shields inscribed with the words 'with this or upon this' meaning they could only return from battle victorious or dead – the ultimate disgrace was to drop the shield and run. At thirteen they were sent into the countryside to survive on their own and kill if necessary. It was this upbringing which made them such legendary fighters.

☆ FIRST recorded battle on English soil

Julius Caesar, Dover (Porta Dubris). 15:00 Friday 26 August 55BC

Julius Caesar was convinced that England was a major source of gold, silver and freshwater pearls, so on 26 August 55 BC, 'at the third watch' (just after midnight), he set sail from Gaul for England with an armada of warships and eighty transport ships carrying two legions and about 10,000 infantry. At 09:00 the fleet sighted local warriors armed with javelins on the cliff tops at Dover. Caesar waited for advantageous conditions before finally beaching his galleys at 15:00 at Walmer, about seven miles from Dover. The hesitant troops were rallied by the eagle bearer of the Tenth Legion who jumped ashore first, shouting: 'Leap, fellow soldiers, unless you wish to betray your eagle to the enemy. I, for my part, will perform my duty to the republic and to my general.' After putting up fierce opposition the British were eventually subdued with *catapultae* and slings fired from the Roman warships, but managed to flee to safety because the transports carrying Caesar's cavalry had been delayed by adverse winds. There followed a series of land engagements with victories going to both sides before the Romans eventually gained the upper hand. Caesar began negotiating peace terms but realised that to complete the subjugation of the British he needed to return with a larger force, which he did with great success the following year – though he never did find the legendary gold, silver and freshwater pearls.

DID YOU KNOW?

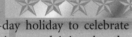

Senators in Rome decreed a twenty-day holiday to celebrate Caesar's victory over the British, despite complaining that the slaves Caesar brought back were worthless since they were neither musicians nor secretaries.

✳ LAST Viking invasion of England

Battle of Stamford Bridge, Yorkshire. Monday 25 September 1066

On the death of Edward the Confessor in 1066 four men claimed the English throne: William, Duke of Normandy; Harold Hardrada, King of Norway; Tostig, the banished Duke of Northumberland; and Tostig's brother Harold Godwinson, Earl of Wessex, who was crowned Harold II the day after Edward's death. While Harold was guarding the south coast against a Norman invasion Hardrada landed on the Yorkshire coast with his Viking army and marched inland to join forces with Tostig. Harold made a six-day forced march northwards and surprised Hardrada at Stamford Bridge, close to York, before Hardrada could organise his defence. Harold's crack troops, trained to wield two-handed axes that could slice through a horse and rider with a single blow, defeated the 10,000 Vikings and both Hardrada and Tostig were killed. However, William landed on the south coast at Pevensey just three days later, and Harold's army was forced to march 241 miles south again to meet the challenge (*see following entry*).

✳ LAST successful invasion of England
☆ FIRST decisive cavalry battle on English soil
☆ FIRST English king to die in battle

Battle of Hastings, Senlac Hill, Battle, Sussex. 08:00 Saturday 14 October 1066

Despite proving himself a formidable commander at the Battle of Stamford Bridge (*see previous entry*), the sovereignty of Harold II, 'the last English king', was to be decided by the Battle of Hastings. On 28 September 1066 William, Duke of Normandy, who had a rival claim to the English throne, landed unopposed at Pevensey with an immense expeditionary force including some 6,000 horses. Legend has it that William tripped as he set foot on the beach but turned the ill omen to his advantage by rising with his hands full of sand shouting: 'I now take hold of the land of England!' The Battle of Hastings didn't actually take place in Hastings – while William set up camp at Hastings, Harold marched south and made his stand on a ridge at Senlac Hill, some six miles north (now within the town of Battle). The Saxons spent the night before the battle drinking and singing while the Normans spent the night confessing their sins. Numerically the English forces were slightly superior (estimates give 7,000 Saxons facing 6,000 Normans) and they held the high ground but the Saxons were exhausted by the gruelling march south and the Normans had a secret weapon: cavalry – the Saxons had never faced a mounted charge. The opposing forces made visual contact at about 08:00. Legend has it that William's minstrel and knight, Ivo Taillefer, begged for permission to strike the first blows of the battle and rode before the Saxons alone, tossing his sword and lance in the air and catching them while he sang an early version of 'The Song of Roland'. A Saxon champion challenged him, but was quickly dispatched by Taillefer who decapitated him and held the head high to show that God favoured the French. Three times the Normans charged the Saxon shield wall and three times they recoiled, the Saxons shouting their defiance with 'Olicrosse!' (holy cross) and 'Ut, ut!' (out, out), and the Normans responding with 'Dex aie!' (God is our help). But the French repeatedly used feigning tactics to wear down the English – the Norman cavalry would attack then feign a retreat before swinging round and slaughtering the separated English pursuers. William had three horses killed under him and once he was thought to be dead but removed his helmet and shouted 'Look, I am alive.' The battle raged for an incredible six hours – the longest of any medieval encounter – and was still undecided. As the aggressor in a foreign land William knew he must secure victory by nightfall in order to survive, and as dusk approached he rallied his troops for a final attack – at last the Saxon shield wall was breached and the Normans slaughtered Harold's bodyguard. The French archers began to shoot their arrows high and at this point one fatally struck Harold in the eye. Accounts differ: some say that he tore out the arrow and continued to fight until cut down by a knight, another that as he tried to pull it out he was cut through the heart by a Norman knight, after which others cut off his head, spilled his guts, and cut off his left leg at the thigh. Whatever the truth, his death signalled the end of the battle, many of the fleeing Saxons being hacked down by pursuing Normans. On Christmas Day William was crowned England's third king of 1066, prompting a lasting change in the nature of English nationality; it was the last time England was conquered by a foreign power.

DID YOU KNOW?

On the day after the Battle of Hastings (*previous entry*) Harold's mother Gytha offered William the Conqueror Harold's weight in gold if he would allow her to bury him in consecrated ground. William refused, declaring that Harold should be buried on the shore of the land which he sought to guard, and ordering that the corpse be buried on the coast under a cairn of stones. Harold's horribly mutilated corpse, with its unrecognisable mangled face, was identified by his first wife Edith Swan-Neck 'by marks on the body, known only to her' – traditionally believed to be a chest tattoo of her name.

❑ ONLY military campaign settled by a game of chess

Seville, Spain. 1078

King Alfonso VI of Castille and his Christian forces were about to besiege the Moors in Seville, who were ruled by al-Mutami. Aware that Alfonso was a great chess player, al-Mutami suggested that if Alfonso could beat the Seville champion Ibn-Ammar, he would surrender the city – but if Alfonso lost he was to withdraw. Alfonso accepted the challenge. He lost the game but kept his word and withdrew his troops without a fight.

❑ ONLY besieged army entirely saved by women

Weinsberg, Germany. Saturday 21 December 1140

After a long siege, King Conrad III forced the surrender of Weinsberg Castle in Heilbronn, Germany. He ordered the execution of all the male defenders of the castle but gave his word that the women were free to leave, promising that they may carry their most beloved possessions with them on their backs. The women chose to carry their husbands out of the castle, infuriating Conrad who nonetheless allowed them to go, saying that a king's word should never be altered. The women came to be known as the *Treue Weiber von Weinsberg* ('Faithful Wives of Weinsberg'), and the castle is nowadays known as *Weibertreu* ('Women's Faithfulness'). During the Second World War, Weinsberg was the site of a prison camp for Allied officers, and on 12 April 1945 the town was destroyed in a massive Allied air raid.

✱ LAST act of mercy by Richard the Lionheart

Chalus-Chabrol Castle, Poitou, France. Thursday 25 March 1199

In March 1199 Richard besieged the unarmed and militarily insignificant castle of Chalus-Chabrol because it was rumoured there was a hoard of Roman treasure within. On 25 March, just prior to the main assault, Richard rode around the castle perimeter inspecting his forces, contemptuously refusing to wear armour despite the occasional arrow being shot from the castle – Richard even sarcastically applauded defenders who loosed arrows in his direction. But, almost inevitably, he was hit by an arrow which struck him in the shoulder near the neck. He retired to his tent where his notoriously unskilled surgeon, nicknamed 'The Butcher', extracted it but mangled Richard's arm in so doing. The signal for the assault was immediately given, the castle was quickly taken by storm, and those defenders who hadn't died fighting were hanged as robbers who had attempted to steal the treasure – all except Bertram de Gourdon, who had fired the fatal arrow and who turned out to be a boy. He was brought before Richard who asked, 'What harm have I done you, that you have killed me?' Bertram defiantly told Richard that he killed him in revenge for Richard personally killing his father and two brothers, adding: 'Therefore take any revenge on me that you may think fit, for I will readily endure the greatest torments you can devise.' Impressed, Richard, as a last act of mercy, forgave the boy and ordered him to be freed and sent away with 100 shillings. Richard's wound swiftly became gangrenous and he died on Tuesday 6 April 1199 in the arms of his mother. Sadly, Richard's last act of chivalry was futile. On his death his captain Mercadier, who had secretly detained Bertram, had him flayed alive and his body torn apart by horses.

DID YOU KNOW?

At six feet five inches, King Richard I, aka Richard the Lionheart, was the tallest English king. In the eyes of his countrymen he was a swashbuckling hero but the fact that he was a homosexual cannibal who spent only three months of his reign in England is rarely mentioned. Described as 'a bad son, a bad brother, a bad husband, and a bad king', he was nonetheless a great warrior who loved fighting. After his death at Poitou (*above*) Richard's brain was buried at the abbey of Charroux in Poitou, his heart at Rouen Cathedral and the rest of his body in Fontevraud Abbey, Anjou. In 1838 a silver box was found at Rouen containing Richard's heart 'reduced to the semblance of a dry, reddish leaf'.

☆ FIRST major naval battle won by an English fleet
☆ FIRST smokescreen

Dover, English Channel. Thursday 24 August 1217

Although outnumbered five to one, the English fleet, commanded by Hubert de Burgh, won a spectacular victory over Eustace the Monk's French fleet by a clever trick. The English totally out-manoeuvred the French by suddenly sailing to windward and pouring huge amounts of quicklime into the sea, creating the first smokescreen in history. They then cut down the blinded French forces and captured 55 enemy ships. This rout of the French Fleet was England's first major naval victory and established her reputation as the ruler of the seas.

☆ FIRST military use of the word 'kamikaze'

Kublai Khan's navy. Thursday 14 August 1281

The Mongols launched two unsuccessful invasions of Japan, the first in 1274 and the second in 1281. On the second attempt the Mongols set out with a vast fleet of 3,500 ships carrying 100,000 men but as the fleet approached Japan on the night of 14 August a devastating typhoon struck, totally destroying the Mongol navy but miraculously leaving the Japanese navy untouched. The Japanese put the success down to the kamikaze or 'divine wind', a name adopted by Japanese suicide pilots in the Second World War.

☆ FIRST use of 'schiltrons'
☆ FIRST major battle decided by the longbow

Battle of Falkirk, Scotland. First War of Scottish Independence. Tuesday 22 July 1298

In the early hours of 22 July 1298 King Edward I's page fell asleep, allowing his master's great warhorse freedom to roam. Unfortunately it trampled on the sleeping 58-year-old monarch, breaking two of his ribs. Another chronicler claims the horse panicked as Edward was mounting it, kicking him and breaking two ribs, but whatever the reason for the broken ribs Edward, in obvious pain, mounted the horse and led his troops to the Battle of Falkirk – although the question of where the battle actually took place is a matter of considerable controversy, with at least seventeen locations suggested. Edward's army of 2,500 cavalry and some 15,000 infantry (many of them archers) vastly outnumbered William Wallace's Scottish forces of 200 cavalry and less than 10,000 infantry. For the first time Wallace formed his infantry into bristling, impenetrable, defensive circles known as schiltrons which, from above, looked like hedgehogs with the soldiers' pikes poking out like quills. Wallace took personal charge and ordered his men to 'dance as best you can'. The schiltrons were so successful in withstanding the cavalry charges that Edward changed tactics, ordering his newly-established longbow men to rain arrows down on them. These storms of arrows were so deadly that it was said each longbow man carried a dozen Scots' lives under his belt. Joining in the rout, the English foot soldiers advanced towards the schiltrons throwing stones and rocks, and the combined hail of arrows and rocks completely smashed the Scottish ranks. The bloodiest battle of the Scots War and first great victory of the longbow ended with the Scots losing forty cavalry and 5,000 infantry compared with just 200 English cavalry killed or wounded – but despite the decisive English victory Wallace managed to escape and continue his defiance.

DID YOU KNOW?

The longbow proved to be the machine gun of the Middle Ages, firing arrows at up to 100mph and delivering blows as forceful as a sledgehammer which could pierce armour at 200 yards. In battle a skilled longbow man would be armed with five or six dozen arrows and could fire ten aimed arrows per minute – so fast that 'it seemed as if it snowed'. The problem of arrow supply was solved by boy runners desperately trying to keep pace with the action. This formidable weapon was known as the 'English Longbow' despite being developed by peasants in Wales.

☆ **FIRST** use of guns in a major European battle
☆ **FIRST** major success for the longbow in Continental warfare

Battle of Crécy, near Crécy-en-Ponthieu, Picardy, France. Hundred Years' War. 18:00 Saturday 26 August 1346

'England's greatest victory over France' is how Winston Churchill described the Battle of Crécy, in which Edward III's estimated 10,000 English soldiers routed Philippe VI's estimated 40,000 French troops. One of the main reasons for this astounding success was that Edward III encouraged the English to practise archery (discouraging tennis, dice, cock fighting and especially football, which often led to rampaging hooligans and mob riots) whereas the French banned peasants from owning arms. Although this was the first occasion gunpowder weapons were deployed on a European battlefield, it is generally acknowledged that the English fired only a few rounds which had no significant influence on the outcome of the battle. In fact Edward, who watched the battle from the safety of a windmill, had only three unreliable mortars, each firing three-inch diameter stone or iron balls, the sound of which was more frightening than the damage they caused. Between 18:00 and 22:30 the English successfully repulsed up to fifteen French charges, and when Edward's sixteen-year-old son – known as the Black Prince because he wore black armour – seemed trapped, his father refused to send reinforcements, saying: 'Let the boy win his spurs for I want him, please God, to have all the glory.' Eventually reinforcements were sent, only to find the teenager and his companions surrounded by the corpses of the French warriors they had slain. When the prince was presented with the crest of the fallen King John of Bohemia he immediately adopted the three white ostrich feathers and John's motto *Ich dien* ('I serve'), which remain to this day the emblem and motto of all Princes of Wales. English losses were fewer than 1,000 dead compared with French losses of 1,542 knights and noblemen plus 10,000 lesser ranks – a greater number than the entire English army. The flower of French chivalry had been wiped out by what the French had dismissed as a 'faint hearted rabble' but which in truth was a highly trained and disciplined infantry, marking the end of the age of chivalry and the mounted knight.

❏ ONLY blind commander never to lose a battle
❏ ONLY commander to become a drum
☆ FIRST commander to use hand guns on the battlefield
☆ FIRST commander to train his men to aim firearms from the shoulder

Jan Zizka. Wednesday 11 October 1424

Zizka was a Czech general and commander of the Hussites (early Protestant Republicans). As a child he lost one eye in a fight – some sources claim he lost it at the Battle of Gunwald – before going on to become a military mastermind and of the few army leaders never to have lost a battle. In 1421 Zizka lost his other eye while besieging the castle of Rabi, but despite now being totally blind he continued to command his forces. He was both unconventional and innovative, and was equally happy leading trained soldiers or inexperienced peasants. He ordered the peasants to arm themselves with threshing tools made lethal with nails, and taught them how to turn their wooden wagons into mobile forts, with mounted cannon and muskets firing through loopholes – presaging the armoured tank five centuries ahead of its time. Zizka would drive the wagons into impregnable circles, creating havoc among attackers, and was apparently able to execute complex manoeuvres at full gallop. He was so respected and admired that after he died of the plague on 11 October 1424 his soldiers called themselves orphans. Zizka's last wish was for his skin to be made into a drum so that he could lead and inspire his troops even after his death. In Prague stands a hilltop monument with a 27-foot statue of Zizka astride a horse – the largest equestrian statue in the world.

* LAST English king killed on a battlefield
* LAST charge of mounted knights

King Richard III, Battle of Bosworth, two miles south of Market Bosworth, Leicestershire. Monday 22 August 1485

Richard III was the third and last English king to die in battle, the first being Harold II at Hastings (*see 1066*) and the second being Richard I at the siege of Chalus-Chabrol Castle (*see 1199*). Although the Battle of Bosworth lasted a mere two hours it was one of the most significant in English history, being the last exchange of power in the long-running civil Wars of the Roses and the start of the Tudor dynasty. Henry Tudor, with only a minor claim to the throne, landed on 7 August at Milford Haven, Wales, with a tiny army of only 2,000 (most of whom were French convicts offered a free pardon if they fought with the would-be usurper) but by the time he arrived unopposed in the Midlands his ranks had swelled to an estimated 5,000 men. Richard III commanded nearly 8,000. In addition there was a third army on the battlefield comprising 3,000-4,000 troops led by Sir William Stanley, whose son Richard held hostage in order to ensure Stanley's support. Richard's enemies claimed he was a hunchback but there can be no doubting his physical strength and courage. With the battle in the balance Richard spotted Henry Tudor cut off from his men with only a few bodyguards, and decided on a do or die assault. On his white horse Surrey, he led a charge of knights, hoping to engage Henry in personal combat, and despite breaking his lance he personally hacked down Henry's standard bearer, Sir William Brandon. But at this crucial moment Stanley made his move and committed his troops to Henry's rescue. Stanley's men overwhelmed the trapped Richard, whose standard bearer, Sir Percival Thirwall, had both legs hewn away but refused to let the banner fall, until he was hacked to pieces. Richard made his last stand alone, on foot, still bravely trying to reach Henry before being pole-axed by a Welsh halberdier. Sir William Stanley found the English crown in a hawthorn bush and placed it on the head of the new king, Henry VII. This marked the beginning of the 118-year Tudor dynasty and is the reason the Tudor emblem is a crown and bush.

DID YOU KNOW?

On the eve of the Battle of Bosworth (*above*) Richard suffered nightmares with visions of 'terrible devils' threatening to tear him to pieces. Unable to sleep, he arose and discovered one of his guards asleep so he stabbed him, saying: 'I found him asleep, and have left him as I found him.' After the battle Richard's battered and naked corpse was trussed over a horse and ignominiously paraded through the streets of Leicester where it was accidentally crushed on the side of a bridge over the River Soar. After being on public display for two days his remains were buried in the church of the Grey Friars, which later became the city's cathedral. The cathedral was destroyed during the dissolution of the monasteries, and if Richard's remains are still at the site then it is sad to report the last Plantagenet King of England lies beneath a municipal car park.

❑ **ONLY** country whose entire military consists of foreign-born soldiers

Papal Swiss Guard, Vatican, Rome. Thursday 22 January 1506

The famous Papal Swiss Guard (Päpstliche Schweizergarde), the world's oldest existing military corps, consists mostly of German-Swiss mercenaries who serve as bodyguards, ceremonial guards and palace guards. The guard was founded in 1506 after Pope Julius II asked the Swiss Diet for a permanent protective force – as a result, 150 Swiss Guards marched across the Alps under the command of Kaspar von Silenen and arrived in Rome to take up duties on 22 January. At the end of 2005 there were 134 members comprising a Commandant (bearing the rank of 'oberst', or Colonel), a chaplain, three officers, one sergeant major ('feldwebel'), thirty NCOs, and ninety-nine 'halberdiers' – a rank equivalent to private, so-called because of the traditional halberd that they carry. Although it is the world's smallest army the Swiss Guard boasts an intelligence service rivalled only by Israel's Mossad. To enlist, one must be Swiss, of legitimate birth, Roman Catholic, single, celibate, aged between nineteen and thirty, have no criminal record and be at least five feet eight inches tall. Once a guardsman achieves the rank of corporal he is allowed to marry. New guards are sworn in on 6 May (the anniversary of the Sack of Rome; *see 1527*) in the San Damaso Courtyard within the Vatican, swearing an oath in German to 'serve the Pope to the death'. A common misconception is that the uniform – in the yellow, blue and red of the Medici family – was designed by Michaelangelo, but in fact the current uniform was the creation of Commandant Jules Repon in 1914. Switzerland still bars its citizens from military engagement other than in the service of the Vatican.

* LAST Scottish king to offer battle in England
* LAST Scottish king to die in battle
☆ FIRST war memorial church window

James IV, Battle of Flodden, Branxton Heath, Northumberland (aka Battle of Branxton). 16:00–c18:00 Friday 9 September 1513

With some 20,000 soldiers on each side Flodden was the largest battle ever fought between England and Scotland, and it ended in a bloody defeat for the Scots. The English were led by the rheumatic, seventy-year-old Earl of Surrey (King Henry VIII was fighting in France) and the Scots by James IV. The weather was wet and stormy, making visibility poor and reducing the power of the English longbows by soaking the strings – despite which the Highlanders were soft targets because few of them wore armour. The rain also made it almost impossible for the soldiers to keep their footing on the already boggy ground, having a worse effect on the Scottish infantry, with its 22-foot pikes, than on the English with its more manoeuvrable 8-foot halberds. Meanwhile, the new Scottish artillery was quickly subdued by the superior English guns. The Scottish leaders fought in the front ranks while the English commanded from the rear, Surrey directing the battle from the luxury of his coach well behind his men. Ignoring his noblemen's advice to follow Surrey's example, King James heroically but rashly led his column so deep into English territory he was killed within a spear's length of Surrey's coach. At a cost of some 1,500 dead the English had inflicted absolute defeat on the Scots – as well as the king, Scotland lost 'the flower of her nobility': James's son Alexander, nine earls, fourteen lords and several highland chiefs. In addition, some 10,000 soldiers were killed, and it was claimed that there wasn't a family in Scotland that hadn't lost a father, husband or son, all of them commemorated in the song and pipe tune 'The Flowers of the Forest'.

DID YOU KNOW?

Sir Richard Assheton recruited many of the Flodden longbow men from Middleton in Lancashire. To commemorate their safe return he rebuilt St Leonard's, the local parish church, and installed England's first war memorial window, the 'Flodden Window', depicting each of the archers by name in stained glass.

❑ ONLY fatalities suffered by the Papal Swiss Guard

Sack of Rome, Vatican, Rome. 06:00 Monday 6 May 1527

On 6 May 1527 troops of Holy Roman Emperor Charles V (who was also King Charles I of Spain) attacked Rome and tried to kill the Pope. The Papal Swiss Guards fought a heroic last stand on the left side of St Peter's Basilica, close to the Campo Santo Teutonico (German Graveyard): 147 of the 189 guardsmen died fighting but gave sufficient time for the other 42 guards to escort Pope Clement VII to safety through the Passetto di Borgo, a secret corridor which still links the Vatican to Castel Sant' Angelo. The courage of those who died is commemorated annually on 6 May, when new recruits are officially sworn in promising, if needs be, to give up their life to protect the Pope as their forebears had done.

❑ ONLY battle in which both leaders fought front line engagements and both were captured by the enemy

Battle of Dreux, France. Saturday 19 December 1562

One of the bloodiest battles of the sixteenth century was fought between 16,000 Catholics led by Anne de Montmorency and Francis, Duke of Guise, on the one hand, and on the other 13,000 Huguenots commanded by Louis I, Prince of Condé, and Gaspard de Coligny. Instead of controlling the battle from a safe distance, both Montmorency and Louis displayed great courage by acting as cavalry brigadiers in the front line – but their courage/recklessness cost them dear when each was taken prisoner by the other's army, leaving the battle in disarray. Both sides suffered heavy casualties, but the Huguenots eventually retreated, giving victory to the Catholics.

✳ LAST major naval battle fought solely between rowing vessels
☆ FIRST ship sunk by gunfire

Battle of Lepanto, Gulf of Patras, Ionian Sea, near Lepanto, Greece. 12:00-17:00 Sunday 7 October 1571

This battle for the ownership of Cyprus, the biggest naval engagement ever fought in the Mediterranean, was fought between Ottoman Turks and a coalition of Christian states known as the Holy League. The Holy League's fleet of 206 galleys and six galleasses (large converted merchant galleys carrying substantial artillery) was commanded by 24-year-old Don John (or Don Juan) of Austria, and faced an Ottoman fleet of 230 galleys and 56 galliots (small, fast galleys with a single sail, used for chasing and boarding enemy ships) commanded by Ali Pasha. Thousands perished on both sides, the ships being locked together with grappling hooks to allow soldiers to swarm aboard the enemy vessels. Don John's pet marmoset spotted a grenade land on the deck of his master's ship, grabbed it and threw it overboard; and soldiers on one Turkish galley, having been exhausted of ammunition, pelted their opponents with oranges and lemons. In desperation Ali Pasha offered his Christian galley slaves their freedom if they would fight for the Turks, which proved costly because, once free, the slaves turned against their former masters.

The Christian victory was absolute: 30,000 Turks were killed and 8,000 taken prisoner; eighty ships were destroyed and 130 captured. The Holy League lost some 15,000 men (but gained 15,000 slaves freed from the Turkish ships) and lost fifty ships. Meanwhile, hundreds of miles away in the Vatican, Pope Pius V interrupted a meeting of treasury officials at 17:00 and declared: 'We must go and give thanks to God. Victory has gone to the Christian fleet.' How he knew this no one knows, but two weeks later a messenger arrived with news of the victory. The official report stated that the battle was won at 17:00 – the exact moment of the Pope's declaration.

DID YOU KNOW?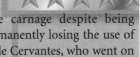

One Spanish soldier survived the carnage despite being wounded twice in the chest and permanently losing the use of his left hand. His name was Miguel de Cervantes, who went on to write what is arguably the world's first novel, centred on one of the greatest characters in literature – the eponymous Don Quixote de la Mancha. As well as the phrase 'tilting at windmills' for facing imaginary adversaries, and the adjective 'quixotic', for an idealistic but unpractical person, the novel also gives another well-known phrase: 'the haves and the have-nots'.

❏ ONLY war started with three men thrown into a pile of manure

Defenestration of Prague, Prague Castle, Bohemia. Thirty Years' War. Saturday 23 May 1618

Defenestration is the act of throwing someone or something out of a window. At Prague Castle on 23 May 1618, a council of Protestants under the leadership of Count Thurn tried two

Catholic Imperial governors, Wilhelm Grav Slavata and Jaroslav Borzita Graf Von Martinicz, for violating the Right of Freedom of Religion. The council found them guilty and threw them, together with their secretary Philip Fabricius, out of the high windows of the Bohemian Chancellery. They all survived unharmed after landing in a large pile of horse manure, after which the Holy Roman Emperor granted Fabricius the title 'von Hohenfall' ('of Highfall'). Imperial Roman Catholic officials claimed that the three men survived because they had prayed fervently to the Virgin Mary as they fell to earth, and that she was thereby acknowledging the righteousness of the Catholic cause. Protestant pamphleteers, on the other hand, asserted that the men's survival had more to do with the softness of the excrement in which they landed. The Defenestration of Prague was one of the main causes of the Thirty Years' War (1618-48) between Protestants (supported by Catholic France) and the Habsburg rulers of the Holy Roman Empire.

✳ LAST words of King Gustavus II Adolphus of Sweden

Battle of Lützen, fifteen miles south-west of Leipzig. Thirty Years' War. Friday 16 November 1632

The Thirty Years' War was an intermittent power struggle between Protestants and the Habsburg rulers of the Holy Roman Empire. The Battle of Lützen, which was fought near Leipzig in Saxony, was a hard-won Swedish victory against an Imperial army commanded by Albrecht von Wallenstein. The battle cost the life of the Swedish king Gustavus Adolphus (aka Gustav Adolf), a military genius who made Sweden the strongest power in Europe. Refusing to put on his armour, Gustavus led a cavalry charge while shouting his last words: 'The Lord God is my armour!' He was then separated from his men and killed.

❑ ONLY military leader killed with his own wooden leg

Sir Arthur Aston, Siege of Drogheda, Ireland. Tuesday 11 September 1649

The English Civil War was fought between Royalists ('Cavaliers') loyal to King Charles I and Parliamentarians ('Roundheads') supporting Oliver Cromwell's parliament. On the outbreak of war Sir Arthur Aston – a rough, untrustworthy, money-grabbing, lecherous but much feared professional soldier – offered his services to King Charles I, only to be rebuffed because of his Catholicism. When Parliamentary chief Lord Fairfax allegedly accepted Aston's tentative offer to fight for parliament, the Royalists forgot their religious differences and appointed him Sergeant-Major-General of Dragoons and later governor of Oxford. In the latter capacity he was described as 'a testy, froward, imperious and tirannical person, hated in Oxon and elsewhere by God and man', and in February 1644 he was confined to his rooms for beating the mayor. On 19 September 1644 he broke his leg in a riding accident – not in battle but 'kervetting on horseback on Bullington Green before certaine ladies'. Gangrene set in and on 7 December his leg was amputated and replaced with a wooden leg in which he reputedly carried gold pieces. On 24 August 1649 Aston was appointed governor of Drogheda, a strategic Irish town protected by a twenty foot wall with 29 guard towers. Aston boasted that anyone who could take Drogheda could capture hell itself but he hadn't counted on Cromwell, who personally led a siege of the town with 12,000 men. On 11 September 1649 Parliamentarian cannon fire breached the walls, and as the Roundheads poured in Cromwell personally forbade any quarter. Aston and 300 members of the garrison made a valiant but hopeless last stand during which Aston had his brains beaten out with his own wooden leg. The leg proved empty but 200 gold pieces were found secreted in his belt.

✱ LAST pitched battle on English soil

Battle of Sedgemoor, four miles south-east of Bridgewater, Somerset. Monmouth Rebellion. 01:30 Monday 6 July 1685

Sedgemoor is often referred to as the last battle fought on English soil, but that is not quite true: it was the last *pitched* battle fought on English soil. (For the last battle of all *see 18 December 1745*.) James, Duke of Monmouth, was the dashing, first, and most favoured of King Charles II's sons but he was illegitimate, his mother being a prostitute named Lucy Walter. When Charles died with no legitimate heir his brother, a professed Roman Catholic, became King James II and Monmouth, exiled in Holland, decided to return and claim the throne. On 11 June 1685 he landed at Lyme Regis, Dorset, with three ships and 83 men. There he issued a proclamation alleging the government had been changed from a limited monarchy into an absolute tyranny and accused James II of poisoning the late king and usurping the throne. Within twelve hours 1,500 anti-Catholic men had rallied to Monmouth's call, and the numbers were increased by the release of prisoners from the town gaol. He then marched through the West Country gathering support until the night of 5-6 July, when his motley army of 3,500 peasants, armed with scythes and pitchforks, met 3,000 of the king's well-equipped, fully-trained soldiers. The Royalists, commanded by Lord Feversham and Lord John Churchill (later Duke of Marlborough), camped at the village of Weston Zoyland and Monmouth decided to gamble everything on a surprise night attack across Sedgemoor. He succeeded in leading his army in silence across the desolate marshland, which was criss-crossed by great drainage ditches, but at 01:30, only 250 yards from the unsuspecting enemy, one of his men's guns accidentally discharged, revealing the rebels to the regulars. A confused order sent Monmouth's infantry and cavalry both into the same deep irrigation ditch, where they crashed into each other and made easy targets for the Royalist cracksmen. Sporadic firing continued for ninety minutes, then Feversham called a halt until daylight, by which time Monmouth had already fled the field. At dawn Feversham's men went in for the kill – 400 rebels had been killed in the battle and 1,000 more in the pursuit, compared with just 80 Royalist deaths and 200 injured. Those rebels that survived the slaughter were bought before the savage Judge Jeffreys' Bloody Assizes, during which Jeffreys sentenced 333 alleged rebels to death and 814 to transportation. By a bizarre twist of fate a well-attested prophecy made c1672 had warned Monmouth 'Beware of the Rhine.' He naturally assumed it meant the German river and made a point of never going near it – little did he know that the Somerset word for a ditch, like the one which cost him the battle and his life, is 'rhine'.

DID YOU KNOW?

Monmouth was discovered three days after the battle hiding in a ditch near Ringwood, Hampshire, disguised as a shepherd having lived by eating raw turnips and peas. He was sent to the Tower of London where, despite humiliating attempts to secure mercy, he was sentenced to be beheaded on 15 July. His last words were: 'Prithee, let me feel the axe. I fear it is not sharp enough. Do not hack me as you did my Lord Russell.' His fears were well founded, because the executioner made such a mess of the job that it took five strokes of the axe and a butcher's knife to sever the head from Monmouth's body. Then someone realised that there was no official portrait of Monmouth, so his head was sewn back on and Sir Godfrey Kneller painted him wearing a handsome neck scarf; the result is on display in Britain's National Portrait Gallery.

☆ FIRST machine gun

James Puckle. Thursday 15 May 1718

On this day English inventor James Puckle patented a portable breech-loading machine gun that could be swivelled and elevated on a collapsible tripod and which, according to the patent, 'discharges soe often and soe many bullets and can be soe quickly loaden as renders it next to impossible to carry any ship by boarding'. The gun had a single barrel behind which was a cylindrical six-chambered magazine turned by a crank handle. There were several magazines to choose from: one fired grenades, another fired standard round shot for use against 'Christian enemies' and a third fired square shot for use against 'heathen Turks.' Although in trials Puckle's gun fired an impressive nine rounds per minute for seven minutes 'despite continuous rain', it attracted little support. To encourage investment Puckle advertised his gun, which he called 'Defence', with the slogan:

> Defending King George your Country and Lawes is
> Defending Your Selves and the Protestant Cause.

This couplet was satirised in prints and on playing cards. The Second Duke of Montagu took two Puckle machine guns on his disastrous 1718 expedition to St Lucia, and though at one point shares doubled in value to £8 the satirists were proved correct in saying that 'Puckle's Machine' was dangerous only to investors. There is a Puckle machine gun in the Royal Armouries, Leeds.

DID YOU KNOW?

Puckle also invented a patent sword which, he claimed in a letter dated 11 April 1720 to James, First Earl Stanhope, 'was worth a victory to the army first has it'. It didn't make the cut.

❏ ONLY war fought over an ear

The War of Jenkins' Ear. First phase of the War of the Austrian Succession. Tuesday 23 October 1739

Robert Jenkins was an obscure Merchant Navy officer who, in 1731, was master of the trading brig *Rebecca*, bound for Jamaica. On 9 April Spanish coastguards led by Captain Fandino boarded *Rebecca* off Havana on suspicion of smuggling. Jenkins, outraged, swore his cargo was legal but the suspicious Fandino had a rope noosed around Jenkins' neck and had him hauled up the fore yard then dropped down on deck. He still denied smuggling, so the process was repeated twice more. After failing to discover anything, Fandino took hold of Jenkins' left ear and slit it with his cutlass, then another Spaniard took hold of the ear and tore it off. Fandino then gave Jenkins the bloody remains, 'bidding him to carry it to his Master King George'. On return to England the press reported the incident, worsening already sour relations between Britain and Spain, but it took seven years for the full impact of Jenkins' mistreatment to be felt. On 22 March 1738 Jenkins was ordered to attend a Parliamentary committee examining grievances against the Spanish over navigation rights and suspected smuggling. In the event he did not attend, but his pickled ear did – it was exhibited to members of the House of Commons and served as a rallying call, whipping up war fever against Spain. In reality Jenkins' ear was an excuse for the British to eject the Spanish from the Caribbean, thus making the West Indies British, and opponents of the war suggested that the entire incident was fabricated, and that in fact Jenkins had lost his ear in the pillory. Despite such opposition, unrelenting pressure forced the peace-loving Prime Minister, Robert Walpole, to reluctantly declare war on 23 October 1739, saying: 'They ring the bells now, they will be wringing their hands before long.' The resulting Anglo-Spanish war, which became known as 'The War of Jenkins' Ear', began in 1739 and in 1742 merged into the War of the Austrian Succession, which ended in 1748. It was an inconclusive war highlighted by numerous inconsequential naval actions (and, ironically, enormous privateering by both sides) and resulted in little territorial gain for either side. Jenkins himself returned to obscurity.

✳ LAST British king to personally lead his troops into battle

George II, Battle of Dettingen, right bank of the River Main between Aschaffenburg and Hanau, Bavaria, Germany. War of the Austrian Succession. Monday 27 June 1743

Britain's sixty-year-old King George II personally commanded some 40,000 British, Hanoverian and Hessian forces against 30,000 French troops led by Marshal the Duke Adrien de Noaalles. It was a decisive Allied victory during which George lost 2,500 men compared with 5,000 French, many of whom drowned attempting to flee across the Main. During the battle French cannon-fire frightened George's horse which bolted and would have carried him into the French lines had one of his aides not stopped the horse. Dismounting, George said that at least he could trust his own legs not to run away and personally led his infantry on foot, sword in hand, in the final decisive counter-attack, shouting in his guttural German accent: 'Now, boys, now for the honour of England, fire, and behave bravely and the French will soon run.' After the battle George sat down with his son William, Duke of Cumberland (*see 16 April 1746*) to a supper of lukewarm mutton which reminded him so much of home cooking that he agreed to return to England and leave the fighting to his generals. He returned to a hero's welcome and, in memory of the victory, Handel composed his 'Dettingen Te Deum'.

DID YOU KNOW?

During the Battle of Dettingen (*previous entry*), Lt-Col Sir Andrew Agnew of The Royal Scots Fusiliers famously warned his men not to fire until they could 'see the whites of their eyes', but warned 'Better kill them afore they kill you'. After the battle, when King George teased him for letting a French cavalry charge break into his regiment's square, Agnew replied, 'May it please Your Majesty, but they didnae get oot again.'

✱ LAST battle on English soil

Battle of Clifton (aka Battle of Clifton Moor), Cumbria. '45 Rebellion. 17:00-18:00 Wednesday 18 December 1745

The last battle on English soil was actually only a skirmish. It was the only significant fighting on English soil during the '45 Rebellion, in which Jacobites led by James II's grandson Bonnie Prince Charlie, in the name of his father James Stuart, attempted to usurp the Hanoverian King George II. George's son William, Duke of Cumberland, was pursuing the Jacobites north from Derby when they met at the village of Clifton, which comprised 'one street with poor houses and enclosures all made with dry stone walls and thick hedges'. One thousand Jacobites under Lord George Murray faced the same number of Hanoverians and the 'battle' began around 17:00 with confused volleys from both sides and much hand-to-hand hit-and-run fighting. The Hanoverians claimed victory after taking control of Clifton at about 18:00 but in terms of losses the winner was Murray, who only suffered about forty casualties compared with Cumberland's sixty. The only prisoner taken was a footman of the Duke of Cumberland who was returned courtesy of Bonnie Prince Charlie. The Scots retreated north, and dried themselves after crossing the River Esk by dancing to the bagpipes.

✳ LAST pitched battle on mainland British soil

Battle of Culloden. Culloden Field, Drummossie Muir, near Inverness, Scotland. '45 Rebellion. 13:00-13:40 Wednesday 16 April 1746

The last battle on mainland Britain – which decided the civil war between rival factions of the royal family – lasted just forty minutes and was contested by armies led by two twenty-five-year-old cousins. The Jacobites (supporters of James II's exiled son James Stuart, aka 'the King over the water', aka the Old Pretender) were attempting to wrest the throne from the Hanoverian King George II. George's son William, Duke of Cumberland, led 8,000 well-equipped highly-trained Hanoverians against 6,750 starving, poorly-armed Jacobites under his alcoholic cousin Bonnie Prince Charlie (the Old Pretender's son, aka the Young Pretender). The armies faced each other a mere 300 yards apart, the Scots facing into freezing winds gusting snow in their faces. A ripple of Jacobite fire was answered by such a fierce bombardment from the Royal Artillery that most of the Jacobite gun detachments immediately ran, and Charles' groom, standing at his side, was decapitated by a cannonball. While the Highlanders' Pipes defiantly played 'Thigibh an so! Clannabh nan con s'gheibh sibh feoil!' ('Come sons of dogs, and I will give you flesh') their men were being slaughtered at such a terrible rate that the heather was reputedly dyed red with their blood. Forty minutes later the battle was over, with 1,500 Jacobites and a mere fifty Hanoverians dead. But the bloodshed continued even after the battle had been won and lost: Cumberland gave no quarter, ordering that the wounded be finished off where they lay and prisoners executed on the spot. For this savagery he was dubbed 'The Butcher', and whilst the British government named a flower 'Sweet William' in his honour, to this day the Scots call it 'Stinking Billy'.

DID YOU KNOW?

The Jacobite defeat at Culloden (*previous entry*) marked the end of the '45 Rebellion and the end of the long-running Jacobite cause to restore the House of Stuart to the British throne, after which the Hanoverians brutally suppressed the Scottish clan system. Charles Stuart (Bonnie Prince Charlie) escaped the battlefield and survived for five months in Scotland despite a £30,000 reward for his capture. He made his final escape to the continent disguised as Flora Macdonald's maid and spent the rest of his life wandering Europe unsuccessfully trying to revive his cause before dying a penniless drunk in Rome in 1788.

❑ ONLY British soldiers allowed to wear their swords in the mess

Worcestershire Regiment, 29th of Foot. September 1746

One night in September 1746 the officers of the Worcestershire Regiment were at Mess in their station in North America when they were treacherously attacked by Native Americans who had previously pledged their loyalty. The attack was beaten off but, to guard against similar attacks occurring in future, the custom of wearing swords at Mess was instituted. After the Regiment left America the custom continued until c. 1850, when a colonel with little regard for tradition abolished it, conceding only that the Captain of the Week and the Subaltern of the Day could wear their swords at Mess – a custom maintained to this day by all battalions of the Worcestershire Regiment in peacetime. As the only British regiment to be sanctioned to wear swords in the Mess, the Worcestershire has earned the nickname 'The Ever-Sworded 29th'.

❑ ONLY British admiral executed for neglect of duty

Admiral John Byng, HMS Monarch, *Portsmouth Harbour. 12:00 Monday 14 March 1757*

In 1756 Byng was sent with a small, ill-equipped fleet to relieve the island of Minorca, under siege from the French. He was confronted by a huge French fleet and spent some time deciding whether to attack, thus losing the element of surprise. Believing the situation to be hopeless but being under 'Fighting Instructions' – a long out-dated set of rules of battle – he attacked but was outgunned and outmanoeuvred, finally withdrawing on the basis that: 'It is better to leave now than to suffer the loss of the entire fleet.' Reports of his 'lily-livered negligence' preceded him back to England, and on arrival he was arrested and made to run the gauntlet of crowds jeering 'Swing! Swing! Great Admiral Byng!' Indicted for failing to do his utmost to take, sink, burn and destroy ships of the enemy, Byng's defence was that withdrawal was the 'wise and humane' course of action. The court cleared him of cowardice but found him guilty of neglect of duty, for which it reluctantly sentenced him to death. Byng was taken aboard his erstwhile command HMS *Monarch* to await the firing squad, where he was visited by a friend who casually asked 'Which of us is the tallest?' Byng replied 'Why this ceremony? I know what it means: let the man come and measure me for my coffin.' At 07:00 on 14 March his coffin was hoisted on board already inscribed: 'The Hon. John Byng, Esqr. Died March 14th 1757.' Byng refused a blindfold and insisted that he give the order to fire by dropping a white handkerchief, saying: 'As it is my fate, I can look at it and receive it.' When it was explained that the firing squad would be unnerved staring him in the eyes he agreed: 'If it will frighten them, let it be done; they will not frighten me.' Just before noon Byng appeared on the quarter deck where stood nine marines with muskets, drawn up in three rows each of three men. In front of them lay a cushion surrounded by sawdust. 'With stately pace and composed countenance' Byng approached the cushion, knelt down and blindfolded himself. The marines advanced. The front rank knelt, the second crouched above them and the third stood erect. Then came the order: 'Cock your firelocks! ... Present!' Byng held a out white handkerchief, let go, and as it flew away in the wind the marines fired. Byng 'sank down motionless, gently falling on his side, as if still studious to preserve decency and dignity in his fall.' He was fifty-three years old. Many believed he was a scapegoat to distract from the government's disastrous policy failures, and historian J H PLumb wrote: 'Disgrace and death on the quarter-deck were Byng's lot for allowing caution and wisdom to prevail.' Byng lies in the family vault in Bedfordshire beneath a tablet inscribed:

> To the perpetual Disgrace of Public Justice
> The Honourable John Byng Admiral of the Blue
> Fell a Martyr to Political Persecution
> On March 14th, in the Year 1757
> When Bravery and Loyalty Were insufficient Securities
> for the Life and Honour Of a Naval Officer.

❑ ONLY British regiment to allow saluting by all ranks even when not wearing any head-dress

Royal Horse Guards ('The Blues'), Battle of Warburg. Seven Years' War. Thursday 31 July 1760

On 31 July 1760 the Marquis of Granby, colonel of 'The Blues', lost his hat and wig whilst leading a charge against the French, thus giving rise to the expression 'going at it, bald-headed'. Forgetting his lack of head-dress, Granby saluted his Commander-in-Chief Prince Ferdinand when reporting his success, and since that day

'The Blues' has been the only regiment to allow saluting by the ranks (but not officers) even when not wearing any head-dress. The tradition continued even after the amalgamation of the Blues with the Royals in 1969.

DID YOU KNOW?

After his military campaigns the marquis (*previous entry*) set up those of his senior NCOs who had been disabled in action as innkeepers, which accounts for the large number of inns throughout the country that bear the name Marquis of Granby.

☆ FIRST shots fired in American War of Independence

Lexington Green, Massachusetts. Wednesday 19 April 1775

'The shot that was heard around the world', and which led to history's most far-reaching revolution, should have never been fired. Acting on information from spies, British general Thomas Gage sent 700 men under marine Major John Pitcairn to seize arms and ammunition stockpiled in Concord. But suspicious Americans became aware of their plans and at 22:00 on 18 April, patriot leader Dr Joseph Warren dispatched William Dawes and later Paul Revere to ride through the night to warn the people of Concord and Lexington of the approaching army. (The poet Longfellow immortalised Revere and left Dawes to be remembered only by historians.) Intelligence reports led Pitcairn to expect a force of over 1,000 Americans at Lexington, but at sunrise on 19 April he found himself facing Captain John Parker and about seventy Minutemen (so called because they had vowed to be ready for battle at a minute's notice) made up of farmers, merchants and tradesmen armed with various types of muskets. The Minutemen were assembled on Lexington Green watched by forty to a hundred spectators, and

Parker instructed them: 'Stand your ground; don't fire unless fired upon, but if they mean to have a war, let it begin here.' Pitcairn rode forward and yelled: 'Disperse, you rebels; damn you, throw down your arms and disperse!' After a brief hesitation some of the locals began to drift away, and there the whole confrontation might have ended except that an unidentified person fired a shot. It could have been an American spectator or an impetuous British soldier – to this day no one knows who fired the infamous shot. Pandemonium ensued and the green was quickly engulfed in gun smoke. When it cleared seven Americans lay dead and eleven wounded, one fatally. There was one British casualty – a wounded redcoat named Johnson. The British cheered and marched on to Concord – the American Revolution had begun. The seven American dead, the first to die in the Revolutionary War, were: John Brown, Samuel Hadley, Caleb Harrington, Robert Munroe, Isaac Muzzy, Ashahel Porter, and Jonas Parker. Jonathon Harrington, fatally wounded, managed to crawl back to his home, where he died on his doorstep.

☆ FIRST American navy

Continental Navy. Friday 13 October 1775

The first four ships of the Continental Navy (formed by the Continental Congress, which governed the American colonies during the Revolution) were named for non-Americans: *Alfred* for King Alfred the Great, who founded the British navy between 878-900AD; *Colombus* for Christopher Columbus, who discovered the New World in 1492; *Andrew Doria* for Andrea Doria, a Genoese sailor and contemporary of Columbus; and *Cabot* for Italian navigator John Cabot (real name Giovanni Caboto), who sailed under letters patent from English king Henry VII and became the first European since the Vikings to set foot on the North American mainland. The first US Navy was established on 30 April 1798.

☆ FIRST winners of the Purple Heart

Sergeants Daniel Bissell, William Brown and Elijah Churchill. American Revolution. Friday 9 May 1783

The first American badge of honour for enlisted men and non-commissioned officers was the Order of the Purple Heart. A decoration for 'military merit', it was established by General George Washington on 7 August 1782 at Newburgh, New York: 'The General, ever desirous to cherish a virtuous ambition in his soldiers, as well as to foster and encourage every species of Military Merit, directs that whenever any singularly meritorious action is performed, the author of it shall be permitted to wear on his facings over the left breast, the figure of a heart in purple cloth or silk, edged with narrow lace or binding. Not only instances of unusual gallantry, but also of extraordinary fidelity and essential service in any way shall meet with a due reward.' The first soldiers to be so decorated were awarded their Purple Hearts for meritorious action during the Revolutionary War. Today the award is reserved for those injured in battle.

☆ FIRST air force
☆ FIRST air force commander

Charles Coutelle, Aerostatic Corps of the Artillery Service, Paris. Saturday 29 March 1794

Coutelle perfected a method of inflating balloons without the use of sulphur, supplies of which were urgently required for manufacturing gunpowder by the French Revolutionary armies. For this invention he was chosen to command the world's first air force, which comprised 34 men: himself, two officers, a sergeant-major, four NCOs, twenty-five men and a drummer boy. Their uniform was blue with black trim, adorned by buttons that depicted a balloon and the word 'Aerostier'. The Aerostiers had to wait until early summer to get their first balloon, which they named *L'Entreprenant* ('*The Enterprising*'). During the first trial Coutelle rose to 1,770 feet and, using a telescope, reported that he could observe about eighteen miles. Within weeks the Aerostiers made their first battle trial: an observation flight at Maubeuge (now in Belgium) during which the balloon – with Coutelle manning the two-man car slung beneath – immediately came under fire from Austrian 17-pounder cannons. Coutelle shouted 'Vive la Republique!' as he beat a quick retreat upwards out of firing range. Although the daring and dashing 'Aerostiers' proved exceptionally popular with women they were not so admired by their military contemporaries – Napoleon himself, who became commander-in-chief of the French army shortly after the Battle of Fleurus, was not convinced by aerial warfare, arguing that the balloon company would not be able to react at the speed battle would require. He had the Aerostatic Corps disbanded in 1799 just five years after its foundation. (For the first full military use *see following entry*.)

☆ FIRST military use of an aircraft

Charles Coutelle, Aerostatic Corps of the Artillery Service, Battle of Fleurus, seven miles north-east of Charleroi, Belgium. French Revolutionary Wars. Thursday 26 June 1794

Three months after the trial at Maubeuge (*see previous entry*) Coutelle's Aerostatic Corps travelled twenty miles to Fleurus to engage in battle for the first time. Not wanting to risk a free flight across country during which *L'Entreprenant* might be shot down, and knowing it would take several days to assemble the generator and furnace and then to inflate the balloon at the battlefield,

Coutelle decided to tow *L'Entreprenant* to Fleurus ready inflated. At Fleurus the 52,000-strong Austro-British-Hanoverian army, commanded by Friedrich Josias, Prince of Saxe-Coburg, faced the 73,000-strong French Army of the Sambre and Meuse, led by General Jean Baptiste Jourdan. A French general, Morlot, clambered aboard *L'Entreprenant*'s two-man 'car' alongside Coutelle, who piloted the tethered balloon using flags to communicate orders to his ground crew who would adjust the cables accordingly. Using a telescope and keeping well out of firing range Morlot was able to judge Austrian tactics and, using a bag and cord attached to the balloon's cables, passed messages which enabled the French to counter every Austrian move and win the day. When the Austrian soldiers saw *L'Entreprenant* rising above French lines many were convinced in the truth of rumours that the French Revolutionary Army was 'in league with the Devil himself'.

❏ ONLY sea battle won by cavalry

Sea of Texel, Netherlands. French Revolutionary Wars. Tuesday 20 January 1795

During the winter of 1794–5, Holland's harshest for a century, French general Charles Pichegru struck deep into the Netherlands while fighting the British and Austrians. On 20 January 1795 the sea off the island of Texel (aka Tessel, the largest of the Dutch Frisian Islands) had frozen solid, trapping a fleet of Dutch ships that had anchored there for safety. Pichegru spotted the trapped fleet and, their horses' hooves specially roughed, led his hussars in full charge across the ice where they surrounded and overwhelmed the hapless ships, won an unconditional surrender and captured the entire fleet. For the only time in military history, a cavalry army had conquered a national navy.

✱ LAST invasion of the British mainland

General William Tate, Fishguard, Pembrokeshire, Wales. French Revolutionary Wars. 14:00 Friday 24 February 1797

In 1797 the French revolutionary government devised a ludicrous plan to foment revolution in Britain and make the people rally to the support of their French liberators. The invasion force of four ships and 1,400 troops set sail from Brest on 16 February 1797 under the command of Commodore Jean Castagnier and General William Tate, an Irish-American septuagenarian renegade who had been court-martialled in America for falsifying muster rolls to raise cash. His 'army' was a ragtag collection of irregulars including 800 convicts released on condition they enlist, and his orders were to destroy Bristol, then cross into Wales and march north to take Chester and Liverpool. Wind conditions made it impossible to land near Bristol, so instead, on 22 February, the ships sailed into Fishguard Bay where they were greeted by a single cannon shot. The cannon was merely an alarm for the townsfolk but, thinking he was under attack, Tate withdrew and sailed on until he reached a sandy beach near the village of Llanwnda where the invaders rowed ashore, scaled the cliffs near Carregwastad and camped around a farm house at Trehowel. The ships returned to France to report the successful landing but the invaders had little taste for fighting and instead spent 23 February enjoying themselves with poultry, port wine and brandy salvaged from a wrecked Portuguese ship. Fuelled by alcohol they set off on a looting spree, stealing the plate of Llanwnda Church and using an eight-day clock at Brestgarn Farm for target practice. Meanwhile, two miles away at Fishguard, 650–750 troops were mobilised under Lord Cawdor. But it wasn't Cawdor's troops who terrified the hung-over French into submission the next day – it was the appearance, on the hillside overlooking their encampment, of several hundred angry local women wearing traditional scarlet 'whittles' (cloaks) and tall black felt hats, which made them look like the fiercest regiment of redcoats ever seen. The invasion collapsed, and Tate's force surrendered to Cawdor on Goodwick Sands at 14:00 on 24 February. Tate later reported that the British came at them 'with troops of the line to the number of several thousand'.

DID YOU KNOW?

The hero of the invasion (*previous entry*) was 47-year-old Fishguard cobbler Jemima Nicholas, the 'General of the Red Army'. At six feet two inches tall, the hard-drinking feisty widow decided to take on the Frenchies single-handed, and marched out to Llanwnda, pitchfork in hand, and rounded up twelve Frenchmen, taking them into town before promptly leaving again to search for more impudent foreigners.

☆ FIRST graduate of West Point Military Academy

Joseph Gardner Swift, West Point, New York. Tuesday 12 October 1802

Originally West Point was a military post overlooking the Hudson River, under the command of future traitor Benedict Arnold. It was established as a Military Academy by Act of Congress on 16 March 1802, and remains both America's oldest continuously-occupied military post and its oldest military academy. Under its first superintendent, Jonathan Williams, only two students graduated out of the original class of ten: the first was Joseph Gardner Swift and the second was Simon Magruder Levy, who became the first Jewish West Point graduate. Both were appointed to the rank of second lieutenant. Levy resigned from the army on 30 September 1805 due to ill health and died in 1807. Swift went on to have an illustrious military career ending as brigadier-general, and in 1816 he became the first West Point graduate to return as head of the academy. He died in 1865. West Point is known as 'The Point' or, less respectfully, by cadets as 'Woo Poo'.

DID YOU KNOW?

George Armstrong Custer (later General) graduated last in his class at West Point. Artist James McNeill Whistler dropped out of the class of 1855. George Patton (later General) was found deficient in mathematics class of 1909 and had to re-enter in order to graduate. Counter-culture icon Timothy Leary dropped out of the class of 1943. Author Edgar Allan Poe was expelled after deliberately neglecting duties, claiming he was too exhausted 'to put up with the fatigues of this place' – he did, however, find the energy to persuade 131 cadets to put up a dollar and a quarter each to finance the publication of his poems.

❏ ONLY meeting of Nelson and the Duke of Wellington

Colonial Office, Downing Street, London. Thursday 12 September 1805

On this day Sir Arthur Wellesley (later Duke of Wellington) went to the Colonial Office for a meeting with Lord Castlereagh, the Secretary of War and the Colonies. As Wellesley entered the ante-room he immediately recognised the great Admiral Horatio, Lord Nelson, but Nelson had no idea that the crop-haired, sunburnt, 36-year-old (ten years younger than himself) was a heroic major-general fresh from nine victorious years in India. Nelson was awkward with strangers and often compensated with outbursts of apparent vanity. Years later, referring to their conversation, Wellington said: 'If I can call it conversation for it was almost all on his side, and all about himself, and really, in a style so vain and silly as to surprise and almost disgust me.' Eventually, something Wellington did or said 'made him guess that I was some-body ...' At that point Nelson excused himself, left the room and established the identity of the young man. He returned, recalled Wellington, 'altogether a different man, both in manner and matter ... certainly a more sudden and compleyte metamorphosis I never saw.' Nelson turned on his famous charm and dazzled Wellington: 'All that I thought a charlatan style had vanished, and he talked of the state of the country and of the aspect and probalities of affairs on the Continent with a good sense, and a knowledge both at home and abroad, that surprised me equally and more agreeably than the first part of our interview had done; in fact he talked like an officer and a statesman.' They talked for almost 45 minutes and Wellington enthusiastically reported: 'I don't know that I ever had a conversation that interested me more,' though, he confessed, 'if the Secretary of State had been punctual, and admitted Lord Nelson in the first quarter of an hour, I should have had the same impression of a light and trivial character that other people have had; but luckily I saw enough to be satisfied that he really was a very superior man.' The meeting was timely. The following day Nelson left London for Porstmouth to embark upon *Victory*, and victory, and death.

✷ LAST words of Nelson

Battle of Trafalgar. 16:30 Monday 21 October 1805

Against all advice, Nelson conspicuously wore all his military decorations during the Battle of Trafalgar as he paced the quarterdeck alongside Captain Hardy. At 13:15 an unknown sniper in the mizzentop of the French ship *Redoubtable* fired his 44.5-inch infantry musket at Nelson some seventy feet below. The musket ball slammed into Nelson's shoulder and through his lungs before splitting his spine and lodging in his back. He slumped to his knees with one hand pressing on the deck, then his arm gave way and he fell on his side. Hardy instantly shouted orders for Nelson to be carried below to the orlop deck, where he died a long slow, agonising death that took three and a quarter hours. He was aware of his condition from the start, saying to the surgeon: 'Ah! Mr Beatty! You can do nothing for me. I have but a short time to live: my back is shot through.' Though drowning in his own blood from internal bleeding he refused any pain-killing opium for fear it would make him vomit, and repeatedly told the surgeon to attend to other wounded men. He developed a raging thirst in the stifling heat of the confined cockpit, and frequently called for a drink and to be fanned. After two hours Hardy came below decks to congratulate Nelson on a brilliant victory, reporting that at least fourteen or fifteen French ships had surrendered. Nelson answered, 'That is well but I bargained for twenty,' adding: 'Anchor, Hardy, anchor!' But when Hardy suggested: 'I suppose, my Lord Collingwood will now take upon himself the direction of affairs,' Nelson was angry, saying, 'Not while I live, I hope Hardy!' He tried to raise himself but failed and said: 'No, do you anchor, Hardy.' Hardy asked, 'Shall we make the signal, Sir?' and Nelson replied with his last order: 'Yes, for if I live I'll anchor.' He laid back and told Hardy that in a few minutes he would be no more, adding: 'Don't throw me overboard, Hardy.' The captain answered, 'Oh! no, certainly not.' 'Then,' replied Nelson 'you know what to do. Take care of my dear Lady Hamilton, Hardy; take care of poor Lady Hamilton. Kiss me Hardy.' Hardy obeyed, and after he had kissed him on the cheek Nelson said: 'Now I am satisfied, Thank God, I have done my duty.' Hardy silently looked down on his admiral for a minute or two then kneeled and kissed him on the forehead. Nelson said 'Who is that?' The captain said, 'It is Hardy,' to which Nelson said 'God bless you, Hardy.' Hardy returned to the quarterdeck. It was 16:10.

In unbearable pain Nelson asked his steward to turn him on his side muttering, 'I wish I had not left the deck, for I shall soon be gone.' He turned to the chaplain and said, 'I have not been a great sinner ... Remember, that I leave Lady Hamilton and my daughter Horatia as a legacy to my country: and never forget Horatia.' He then called, 'Drink, drink!' and 'Fan, fan!' before slipping in and out of consciousness, constantly repeating: 'Thank God, I have done my duty.' At 16:25 Beatty could find no pulse but at that moment Nelson opened his eyes, looked up, then closed them again. Five minutes later he died. Although the battle continued for over an hour more Nelson died knowing victory was his.

❋ LAST journey of Lord Nelson

Trafalgar to St Paul's, London. 21 October 1805 to 9 January 1806.

After he was killed at the Battle of Trafalgar (*see previous entry*) Nelson's corpse had to be preserved. The ship's surgeon, Mr Beatty, located the largest barrel on board and two men brought Nelson's five foot six inch corpse to the middle deck and placed it headfirst in the barrel, which was then closed and filled with brandy. On 24 October a terrified guard reported that the lid on the cask was being pushed up from within – Nelson wasn't trying to escape, it was the gasses expelled from his body that were raising the lid. A new hole was made in the cask, the air released and the sentry calmed. The voyage to Plymouth took a month, during which Nelson's body began to absorb the brandy, so the cask was topped up twice with spirit of wine. An autopsy discovered the fatal musket ball two inches below the inferior angle of Nelson's right scapula, attached to a piece of his coat and a considerable amount of gold lace from his epaulette. After the autopsy Nelson was laid in a leaden coffin, filled with brandy holding in a solution of camphor and myrrh. This was placed inside a larger wooden coffin. The last time Nelson was seen was when his body was again removed from the leaden coffin and placed in a wooden one made from the mainmast of French flagship *L'Orient*, which had been given to Nelson as a gift after the Battle of the Nile. All the witnesses confirmed that although his features were slightly swollen from the absorption of the spirits the body was in excellent condition. The body was dressed and laid in state in the Painted Hall at the Royal Naval Hospital in Greenwich before being taken along the Thames for burial in St Paul's Cathedral on 9 January 1806, eighty days after he had been killed. As the flag-draped coffin was being placed in the black marble sarcophagus in which it lies to this day, the sailors who carried it, 'overcome with emotion', seized Nelson's personal flag and tore it to pieces, each keeping a scrap as a personal memento of their hero. The sarcophagus (which literally means 'flesh consuming') had been built for Henry VIII's adviser Cardinal Wolsey but later confiscated by Henry and stored, forgotten until 1805, in Windsor Castle – thus England's greatest naval hero is buried in a second-hand tomb.

✻ LAST naval fleet action under sail

Battle of Navarino, Navarino, Greece. Greek War of Independence. Saturday 20 October 1827

Rarely can such a decisive battle – in which a small allied fleet virtually destroyed the sea power of the Ottoman Empire – have been so unplanned. Twenty-four British, French and Russian ships under the command of Trafalgar veteran Vice-Admiral Sir Edward Codrington were acting as neutral 'policemen' during the Greek struggle for independence from the Turks. Like most Englishmen of the time, Codrington was pro-Greek and kept a strict watch on the joint Turkish-Egyptian fleet of 89 heavily-armed vessels in Navarino Bay while allowing the tiny Greek navy the freedom of the seas. On 20 October 1827, responding to a rumour that the Turkish-Egyptian fleet was about to attack Hydra, Codrington decided to blockade them by taking his own fleet into Navarino Bay. He sent HMS *Dartmouth* ahead to reconnoitre but *Dartmouth* was greeted with musket fire so he sent in a larger ship for support. This too was fired upon, so the main Allied ships returned musket fire; the Egpytian ships replied with cannon fire and the battle was soon under way, developing into four hours of utter confusion, being fought at such close quarters that the heavy smoke from the gunfire reduced visibility almost to nil. But it was discipline and superior gunnery rather than force of numbers which won the day: when the firing stopped, only 29 of the 89 Turkish-Egyptian ships were still afloat, while the Allies had not lost a single ship. In four hours Greece had been saved and her eventual independence from the Ottoman Empire assured. However, despite the gratitude of the Greek nation, Codrington earned a stern reprimand from the British Admiralty, which considered that he had far exceeded his instructions for this 'untoward event', and was relieved of his command (though officially for other reasons). It wasn't until 88 years later, at the Battle of Jutland, that the Royal Navy was next engaged in full fleet action, by which time the sails of the 'wooden walls of England' had been replaced by steam-powered Dreadnought battleships.

❑ ONLY army created as a result of a fly swat
❑ ONLY army to enlist recruits with assumed identities

French Foreign Legion. Wednesday 9 March 1831

In 1827, angered by a financial deal in which he felt he was being cheated by the French government, Khoja Hussein, the last Dey of Algiers, summoned French Consul Pierre Deval, charged him with being a 'wicked, faithless, idol-worshipping unworthy,' and struck him three times with a peacock-feather fly whisk. On 9 March 1831, to help economise on French manpower, King Louis Philippe of France raised 'A legion of foreigners for service outside France', whose first task was to avenge the Fly Whisk outrage. General Louis de Bourmont and 37,000 men headed for Algeria where, within three weeks – despite the Dey insisting that he had only been trying to swat a fly – they were parading in triumph through Algiers to the strains of 'Wilhelm Tell'. Algeria would be the home of the French Foreign Legion for the next 130 years. Legionnaires may enlist under a pseudonym ('declared identity') and a declared citizenship, which means that French citizens may join the 'foreign' legion under a fictitious nationality (generally a francophone one, often that of Monaco), after which their original identity officially ceases to exist. Under French law the Foreign Legion may deny the existence of any serving legionnaire, and any person revealing the true identity of a legionnaire may be prosecuted under civil law. Although legend has it that the legion is open to everyone, convicted felons are generally prohibited from joining.

❑ ONLY wars the British fought for drugs

Opium Wars, 1839–42 and 1856–60.

The opium trade was a hugely profitable venture for British merchants in China from the 1810s but Lin Tse-hsu, the High Commissioner at Canton, considered that the addictive effect on his fellow Chinese amounted to exploitation by the British. He ordered the outlawing of the trade and the confiscation of all opium in Cantonese warehouses. The British, who championed free trade, argued that the Chinese had no jurisdiction over British subjects but the Chinese started executing anyone importing opium. When a local villager was killed by British sailors the Chinese demanded the sailors be brought to trial. The British refused, the Chinese forbade trade with Britain and war erupted. The Royal Navy prevailed over the Chinese and the first Opium War ended with Hong Kong being ceded to the British under the Treaty of Nanjing (Nanking) and five 'treaty' ports being opened to free trade by British merchants: Amoy, Canton, Fouchow, Nangpo and Shanghai. The second attempt by the Chinese to establish local rights ended in the same failure and this time, under the Treaty of Tianjin (Tientsin), the whole of China was opened up to free trade.

❑ ONLY regiment to have been massacred three times

44th Foot, later the Essex Regiment and now the Royal Anglian Regiment, Prestonpans 1745, Monongahela River 1755, and Gandamak 1840.

The first annihilation of Britain's most massacred regiment was on 21 September 1745 at the Battle of Prestonpans, when Prince Charles Edward Stuart's highlanders killed, wounded or captured nearly all the infantry of Lt Col Sir John Halkett's 44th Foot. Almost exactly ten years later, on 9 July 1755, the 44th was part of Major General Edward Braddock's army, which was massacred on the Monongahela River, in what is now Pennsylvania, by Native Americans fighting for France. On that occasion the 44th was again commanded by Halkett (by then a full colonel), who had been taken prisoner at Prestonpans. This time he wasn't so lucky, and was killed along with many of his men including his own son. In August 1840, the 44th was part of General Sale's ill-fated army in the First Afghan War. Sale's army was forced to retreat from Kabul pursued by the Afghans in strength, and at Gandamak, in the Afghan mountains, the 44th Regiment was annihilated for the third time.

✳ LAST use by the Royal Navy of the word 'larboard'

British Admiralty. Friday 22 November 1844

For centuries sailors used the terms 'starboard' for right and 'larboard' for left. 'Starboard' appears to have originated with the Vikings who shipped with their 'star', or 'steering oar' on the right-hand side and because the side of a ship is its 'board', hence 'starboard'. 'Larboard' meant 'loading side', since ships would steer with the right side away from the dock to avoid damaging the oar. Confusion between the two names was rife, especially in bad weather or strong winds. Since boats unloaded cargo from the side nearest the dock, or port, 'larboard' gradually became known as the 'port' side. In 1844 the British Admiralty finally declared: 'As the distinction between starboard and port is so much more marked than between starboard and larboard it is their Lordships' direction that the word larboard shall no longer be used.'

☆ FIRST man to win the VC

Charles Lucas, HMS Hecla, *Aland Islands, Finland. Crimean War. Wednesday 21 June 1854*

The Victoria Cross is Britain's highest military medal. It is only awarded for 'most conspicuous bravery, or some daring or pre-eminent act of valour, self sacrifice or extreme devotion to duty in the presence of the enemy'. The original medals were all cast from gun metal from the cascabels of two cannons captured from the Russians at Sebastopol during the Crimean War. The front is simply inscribed 'For Valour'. On 21 June 1854 the paddle-steamer HMS *Hecla* and two other ships were bombarding Bomarsund, a Russian fortress in the Aland Islands, off Finland. Fire was returned from shore, and at the height of the action a live shell landed on *Hecla*'s upper deck, its fuse still hissing. All hands were ordered to fling themselves flat on the deck, but nineteen-year-old mate Charles Davis Lucas (later Rear-Admiral) ran forward and hurled it over the side, where it exploded with a tremendous roar before it hit the water, slightly damaging the ship and wounding two men. But thanks to Lucas's action no one was killed or seriously wounded. Lucas was gazetted with the award on 24 February 1857, and attended the first investiture in Hyde Park on 26 June 1857, when Queen Victoria decorated 62 officers and men for their actions in the Crimea. Unusually, Lucas was also awarded the Royal Humane Society medal for lifesaving, despite being engaged in warlike activity.

* LAST British brigade cavalry charge
☆ FIRST man killed in the Charge of the Light Brigade

Light Brigade, North Valley, Battle of Balaclava, Crimea, Ukraine, Russia. Crimean War. 11:10 Wednesday 25 October 1854

Tennyson's lines 'Theirs not to reason why / Theirs but to do and die' romantically sum up one of the most costly mistakes in British military history. Fifty-seven-year-old Lord Cardigan, Commander of the Light Brigade, was an arrogant, quarrelsome, pig-headed and rather stupid officer who had purchased his commission and never seen active service. However, he was passionately proud of the 11th Hussars, of which he was colonel and on which he spent £10,000 a year of his own money. His immediate superior was his hated brother-in-law, the imperious, overbearing Lord Lucan, who had the command of the whole Cavalry Division having been recalled for duty after retiring from the army seventeen years earlier. At 08:00 the battle began when 20,000 Russian infantry and 5,000 cavalry attacked British-held Balaclava. The British repulsed the attack but the British commander-in-chief Lord Raglan failed to follow up the advantage and foolishly gave the Russians time to re-form. Raglan surveyed the scene from the 600-foot Sapoune Heights. Immediately below him was the Light Brigade, comprising men from five highly trained cavalry regiments. To his left were the Fedioukine Heights and to the right the Causeway Heights; the valley between was about a mile wide. At the far end of the valley, about one and a half miles away, were twelve Russian field guns protecting the hastily reformed Russian cavalry and infantry. Raglan saw the Russians starting to retrieve their guns from the Causeway Heights to his right and dictated a message to Lucan, taken down in pencil by Quarter-Master-General Richard Airey:

> Lord Raglan wishes the cavalry to advance rapidly to the front, follow the enemy and try to prevent the enemy carrying away the guns. Troop horse artillery may accompany. French cavalry is on your left. Immediate.
> R Airey.

This ambiguous message was delivered by Airey's aide-de-camp Captain Louis Nolan, who despised both Lucan and Cardigan. When Lucan received the message he was confused because from his vantage point he could not see the enemy's strong points. He growled at Nolan: 'Attack, Sir? Attack what?' At this point history blames Nolan for the misunderstanding that caused the Light Brigade to advance at the battery of guns at the end of the valley and not, as Raglan intended, at the more lightly-defended redoubts on the Causeway Heights. Nolan – who would be the first man killed in the charge – gesticulated in the direction of the valley and said: 'There are the enemy, my Lord, and there are the guns.' Lucan understood this to mean he was to order a suicidal charge against the massed guns at the end of the valley. Had he and Cardigan been on better terms they might have discussed the situation but Lucan simply trotted over to Cardigan and repeated Raglan's orders. When Cardigan protested that the Russians not only had guns at the end of the valley but also at the sides Lucan replied: 'Lord Raglan will have it.' At 11:10 Cardigan led three lines of cavalry down the valley, muttering: 'Here goes the last of the Brudenells' (his family name). The first Russian salvo struck when the Light Brigade had travelled only fifty yards, and for the next eight minutes they were under constant bombardment from all sides. Cardigan's courage was undeniable: he rode right through the guns to within a few yards of the Russian infantry massed beyond, while behind him scores of his men were felled. About 500 of the brigade followed Cardigan through the guns and spent about four minutes in hand-to-hand fighting, slashing at the Cossacks guarding the guns. The 2,000-strong Russian cavalry fled, chased by the Light Brigade until Cardigan ordered a return through the 'valley of death' which took about another eight minutes. In just over twenty minutes the 673-strong Light Brigade lost an estimated 113 men, with 134 wounded, 25 taken prisoner and 475 horses killed or later destroyed. (Note: few sources agree on numbers, with some estimating that as many as 478 were killed, wounded or captured and only 195 escaped unscathed.) Lucan was subsequently promoted field marshal and Raglan died in the Crimea the following year. As for Cardigan, as soon as he reached British lines he trotted back to his yacht, took a hot bath, drank a bottle of champagne and went to bed.

DID YOU KNOW?

The Crimean War is the only war to have given rise to the names of three items of clothing: Balaclava to the balaclava helmet (the woollen helmet soldiers wore to keep themselves warm); the cardigan, as worn by Lord Cardigan, and the Raglan sleeve. Other military eponyms include praline, after French Field Marshal Count du Plessis-Praslin, and shrapnel, after English artillery officer Henry Shrapnel, the inventor of the pellet-filled shell.

☆ FIRST camels imported to the US for military purposes

Indianola, Texas. Wednesday 14 May 1856

In 1854 newly-appointed US Secretary of War Jefferson Davis (later president of the Confederacy) was looking for a solution to transport problems in the western US, where the rough terrain and dry climate were deemed too rough for army horses and mules. Camels were suggested, and on 14 May 1856 the US Navy store ship *Supply* arrived at Indianola, Texas, from Smyrna with 34 camels and five drivers. (The camels had been bought in the Mediterranean by Lt David Porter, who made a shrewd purchase: he had paid for 33 but by the time the shipment arrived another had been born.) Lt Edward Fitzgerald Beale took charge, and hired Syrian camel driver Hadji Ali to teach the soldiers how to pack the animals; the soldiers had a hard time pronouncing Ali's name so they nicknamed him Hi Jolly. In June 1857 Beale and Hi Jolly led an expedition from Fort Defiance to the Colorado River – a trailblazing survey whose route eventually became part of the legendary Route 66. The camels proved a great success, and Beale reported: 'The harder the test they (the camels) are put to, the more fully they seem to justify all that can be said of them ... They pack water for days under a hot sun and never get a drop; they pack heavy burdens of corn and oats for months and never get a grain; and on the bitter greasewood and other worthless shrubs, not only subsist, but keep fat ... I look forward to the day when every mail route across the continent will be conducted and worked altogether with this economical and noble brute.' Unfortunately the camels' stubbornness and aggressiveness made them unpopular among soldiers, and they frightened horses. Despite this, in 1858, Secretary of War John Floyd urged Congress to authorise the purchase of 1,000 more camels.

However, Congress was preoccupied with trouble brewing between the North and South, and quickly forgot the idea of the Camel Military Corps. Most of the animals were auctioned off, although a few escaped into the desert where most were shot as pests by prospectors and hunters. Hi Jolly kept a few and started a freighting business between the Colorado River ports and mining camps to the east. The business failed, however, and Jolly released his last camel in the desert near Gila Bend. He died in 1902 and is buried in Quartzsite, Arizona, where his grave is marked by a pyramid-shaped monument topped with a small metal camel.

☆ FIRST black man to win the VC
☆ FIRST Canadian seaman to win the VC

Able Seaman William Hall (later Quartermaster and Petty Officer). Indian Mutiny. Monday 16 November 1857

Nova Scotia-born Hall joined the US Navy at the age of seventeen, serving in the Mexican War before enlisting in the Royal Navy in February 1852 and serving in the Crimean War as part of the Naval Brigade which fought on land and sea. When the Indian Mutiny broke out Hall, serving on board HMS *Shannon*, became part of '*Shannon*'s Brigade' – a land-based force of 250 sailors equipped with naval cannons. The brigade sailed up the Ganges to Cawnpore and then marched to Lucknow, where British troops and East India Company officials and their families were besieged by rebels. Protecting Lucknow was the strongly-defended Shah Nujeff Mosque, which repulsed all attempts by infantry to storm it. The only solution was to destroy the walls using the brigade's cannons. From 350 yards the guns had little effect, so on 16 November 1857 two gun crews were ordered much closer, to the point where they were in danger of bricks flying back off the walls. One of the crews was missing a man and Hall volunteered despite being warned there was a great chance he would be killed. The gun crews kept up a steady fire while a hail of musket balls and grenades from the mutineers inside the mosque caused heavy casualties, killing everyone except Hall and his badly wounded commander, Lieutenant Thomas Young (also awarded the VC). Between them they continued loading and serving the last gun – as long as they stayed close to the wall they were safe from overhead fire but every time the gun was fired the recoil knocked it back into the fire zone. Hall continually dragged the cannon back and forth, firing until the wall was breached – his action was described as 'almost unexampled in war'. Hall retired from the navy in 1876, declining an offer of Whitehall desk job (which would probably have made him the first coloured civil servant), instead returning to Nova Scotia to work as a farmer with his two sisters. Hall died at Hantsport, Nova Scotia, on 27 August 1904 and was buried in a simple ceremony with no gravestone. Forty-one years later, after a public campaign, his remains were reinterred in front of Hantsport Baptist Church, where a cairn was erected in his honour.

❑ ONLY recipient of the Victoria Cross to have held every rank from private to major general

Lieutenant and Adjutant (later Major General) William McBean, Lucknow, India. Indian Mutiny. Thursday 11 March 1858

Forty-year-old Scotsman McBean was serving with the 93rd Regiment, British Army (later Argyll & Sutherland Highlanders – Princess Louise's) during the Indian Mutiny. At the relief of Lucknow he killed eleven Indians using only a rusty knife and his bare fists, and there are reports that he fought five Indians at once, one of them reputedly six feet seven inches tall and 265 pounds. As McBean walked away from the carnage, he was attacked by a twelfth Indian and several men came to his assistance. Telling them not to interfere, he and the havildar fought with swords, McBean evenutally killing the enemy with a blade to his heart. When presented with his Victoria Cross and congratulated on a good day's work, he replied: 'Tutts, it didna tak' me twenty minutes.'

❑ ONLY war caused by a pig

The Pig War, Washington–British Columbia border. Wednesday 15 June 1859

The Oregon Treaty of 15 June 1846 resolved the 'Oregon border crisis' by dividing the hitherto jointly-administered Oregon Territory (which included part of British Columbia and the modern states of Oregon, Washington and Idaho) between the US and Britain. However, there remained some ambiguity over the San Juan Islands, which the British Hudson's Bay Company turned into a sheep ranch but where American settlers also set up home. Exactly thirteen years later, on 15 June 1859, an American farmer named Lyman Cutlar spotted and shot dead a giant black boar eating his potatoes. Unfortunately the pig was owned by Irishman Charles Griffin, who was employed by the Hudson's Bay Company to run the sheep ranch. Cutlar offered Griffin $10 compensation but Griffin demanded $100; Cutlar then argued that the pig had been trespassing on his land and warned Griffin, 'Keep your pigs out of my potatoes!' To which Griffin replied, 'Keep your potatoes out of my pigs!' The situation escalated, and when the British authorities threatened to arrest Cutlar, American settlers called for military protection, which arrived in the form of 66 American soldiers of the 9th Infantry led by a captain, with orders to prevent the British from landing; the British retaliated by sending three warships under the command of a captain. By 10 August, 461 Americans commanded by a colonel were opposed by five British warships under a rear admiral. Both commanding officers had orders not to fire the first shot and for several days soldiers from both sides shouted insults, hoping to goad the others into making the first move. Ultimately no shots were fired and a very friendly joint military occupation was agreed, with the garrisons attending parties to celebrate each other's national holidays and holding highly competitive athletic meetings. On 25 November 1872, after arbitration by Kaiser Wilhelm I of Germany, the British withdrew, but to this day the Union Jack flies above what was the British camp, being raised and lowered daily by park rangers. It is one of the very few places without diplomatic status where US government employees regularly hoist the flag of another country. Although the thirteen-year Pig War involved thousands of soldiers none exchanged shots, and the only casualty was the pig.

☆ FIRST shot of the American Civil War
☆ FIRST man killed in the American Civil War

Edmund Ruffin and Daniel Hough, Fort Sumter, South Carolina. American Civil War. 04:30 Friday 12 April 1861

The American Civil War was fought between the anti-slavery Northern states (the Union) and the pro-slavery Southern states (the Confederation). Fort Sumter, at the mouth of Charleston Harbour, was occupied by a Union garrison, commanded by Major Robert Anderson, comprising 85 officers and men, twelve of whom were musicians. It was surrounded by some 7,000 Confederate troops under General P G T Beauregard, who knew Anderson well as Anderson had taught him artillery at West Point. Although Union President Lincoln promised 'to hold and possess' Fort Sumter no matter what, he made it clear he did not want his men to fire the first shot in anger. Meanwhile Confederate President Jefferson Davis demanded the fort's evacuation or destruction. At 04:30 on 12 April 1861 Beauregard's patience was exhausted – he detailed Lt Henry to fire a signal shell that burst 100 feet above the fort and then ordered that the first shot be fired. The honour of firing the cannon went to 67-year-old Virginian farmer Edmund Ruffin, who wrote in his diary: 'Of course I was highly gratified by the compliment & delighted to perform the service, which I did. The shell struck the fort, at the north-east angle of the parapet' – the Civil War was officially underway. Fort Sumter was pounded with guns and mortars for 34 hours before Anderson was forced to surrender. During that time, miraculously, no soldier was killed. The terms of capitulation allowed Anderson to fire a salute to the US flag and to march out with colours flying. His men fired 49 rounds in salute but the gun firing the fiftieth and last round exploded and killed Private Daniel Hough, who thus became the first fatality of the war. Four years later, on 18 June 1865, Ruffin learned that Confederate General Robert E Lee had surrendered at Appomattox. Devastated, Ruffin sat at his desk and wrote:

> I hereby declare my unmitigated hatred to Yankee rule – to all political, social and business connection with the Yankees and to the Yankee race. Would that I could impress these sentiments, in their full force, on every living Southerner and bequeath them to every one yet to be born! May such sentiments be held universally in the outraged and down-trodden South, though in silence and stillness, until the now far-distant day shall arrive for just retribution for Yankee usurpation, oppression and atrocious outrages, and for deliverance and vengeance for the now ruined, subjugated and enslaved Southern States! ... And now with my latest writing and utterance, and with what will be near my latest breath, I here repeat and would willingly proclaim my unmitigated hatred to yankee rule – to all political, social and business

connections with Yankees, and the perfidious, malignant and vile Yankee race.

Ruffin then swapped pen for gun and shot himself in the head. Thereby, according to some, he fired both the first and the last shot of the American Civil War.

DID YOU KNOW?

By some definitions the first shot was fired on 9 January 1861, when the Confederates fired on the relief ship *Star of the West* attempting to resupply Fort Sumter. This 'first shot' (so-called by some though it did not lead to further hostilities) was fired with a handgun by Confederate Cadet George E Haynesworth. Seventeen shots were fired, and although just two hit the target the *Star of the West* was forced to retreat because Anderson did nothing to assist, as he believed his orders were too vague and his position too precarious to risk starting a civil war.

☆ FIRST Union shot of the American Civil War

Abner Doubleday, Fort Sumter, Charleston Harbour, South Carolina. 07:00 Friday 12 April 1861

It wasn't until two and a half hours after the first rebel fire struck Fort Sumter (*see previous entry*) that Captain Abner Doubleday gave the order to shoot back. The first Union shot 'bounded off the sloping roof of the battery opposite without producing any apparent effect.' Doubleday is better known for supposedly inventing the game of baseball in Elihu Phinney's cow pasture in Cooperstown, New York, in 1839. Many people believe this myth despite the fact that Doubleday made no such claim, and that the story originated with Abner Graves who, after shooting his wife, was committed to an institution for the criminally insane.

❏ ONLY person present at the first and last moments of the American Civil War

Wilmer McLean, Yorkshire, Bull Run, near Manassas Junction in Prince William County, Virginia. 12:00 Thursday 18 July 1861

'The Civil War began in my dining room and ended in my parlor.' Thus, reputedly, spake wholesale grocer Wilmer McLean. McLean was enjoying a peaceful retirement on a Virginia plantation called Yorkshire, but his tranquillity was smashed on 18 July 1861 by the initial engagements of what would become the Battle of Bull Run (aka the Battle of Manassas), the first major battle of the Civil War. Confederate Brigadier General P G T Beauregard had decided to make McLean's house his headquarters, and at noon a Union shell dropped into one of the chimneys, fell into the kitchen fireplace and exploded in a kettle of stew. Casualties from the skirmish were taken to McLean's barn, which continued to be shelled even though it flew the yellow hospital flag. Three days later the full-scale Battle of Bull Run saw 32,000 Confederate troops rout 30,000 Yankees. After the battle had been won and lost, and the armies had left the area, McLean moved well away from war zones, buying a house in the isolated village of Appomattox Court House in southern Virginia. Three years later, at noon on 9 April 1865, his tranquillity was smashed again when Confederate Colonel Charles Marshall marched into the village, saw McLean, and asked where would be a good place for Confederate General Lee and Union General Grant meet to sign the surrender. McLean offered his own home and his front parlour was approved for the historic ceremony, which took place at about 13:30; the surrender was so affable that the generals reminisced about serving together in the Mexican War and 'almost forgot the object of the meeting'. In 1893 the house where the surrender was signed was taken down and transported to

Washington for display but the project was never completed and the fabric of the house was lost forever. In 1948 an exact replica was built, and in 1950 it was dedicated as part of the national park and opened in the presence of U S Grant III and Robert E Lee IV.

DID YOU KNOW?

When Generals Lee and Grant departed after signing the surrender, the trouble began for McLean. War-weary soldiers instantly turned into rampaging souvenir hunters, and when McLean made it clear he didn't want to sell anything they simply left money where household items once stood. After the large items disappeared the house was ransacked, and almost anything that wasn't nailed down vanished. However, two major items were accounted for. General Sheridan obtained the table on which the surrender terms were written and gave it to the wife of General Custer; it now resides in the Smithsonian Museum. The table upon which the surrender was actually signed was obtained by General Ord and is now in display at the Chicago Historical Society. McLean never recovered the financial loss and in 1867, unable to keep up the mortgage, he sold the house and moved back to Bull Run. He died in 1882.

❏ ONLY military order to regard hostile women as prostitutes

Benjamin Butler, New Orleans. American Civil War. Thursday 15 May 1862

On 28/29 April 1862 Admiral David Farragut, assisted by Butler's Union army, captured New Orleans, and on 1 May Butler began his command of the occupied city. The residents of the once-wealthy city made little attempt to disguise their resentment and contempt for the occupiers who had brought them poverty and hardship, and in return Butler made life as difficult as he could for them by placing the whole city under martial law, confiscating all firearms and outlawing public assemblies. The local women were particularly brazen in showing their disgust, and when six women on a balcony collectively turned and aimed their backsides towards Butler, he retorted: 'These women evidently know which end of them looks the best.' However, when a woman in the French Quarter emptied a chamber pot over Farragut's head Butler took more dramatic retaliation – on 15 May he issued General Order No. 28, which became known as the 'Woman Order', announcing that any female who insulted a Union soldier by word or deed would be regarded and held liable as a prostitute (in official terms 'a woman of the town plying her avocation'). This slur on their women's honour outraged the Confederate Southerners, who argued that it encouraged the Unionists to violate the city's women, but Butler insisted that his men would treat all those contravening the order in the same way as would any well-bred person who encountered prostitutes in public – by ignoring them. One Southern newspaper put a $10,000 price on Butler's head and Jefferson Davis, the Confederate president, denounced him as 'brutal'. Across the Atlantic in Britain, where the upper class were sympathetic to the Confederacy, the *Times* thundered that Butler's Woman Order was 'military rule of intolerable brutality'. The prime minister, Lord Palmerston, condemned it as 'infamous', saying: 'Sir, an Englishman must blush to think that such an act has been committed by one belonging to the Anglo-Saxon race.' British Foreign Secretary Lord Russell complained to the American Secretary of State, William Henry Seward, who simply rejected the argument and supported Butler's action. Butler's Woman Order was effective in shaming the white women of New Orleans into suppressing their insulting words and behaviour but in the end it wasn't feminine sensitivity that resolved the situation.

Butler's entire administration was riddled with corruption and Butler himself was nicknamed 'Spoons' for allegedly stealing silverware from the mansions of the wealthy. On 16 December 1862, to the delight of the now-redeemed Southern belles, President Lincoln recalled the shamed Butler as commander of New Orleans and replaced him with General Nathaniel Banks.

☆ FIRST rapid-fire machine gun

Gatling Gun, invented by Richard Jordan Gatling, Indianapolis, USA. US Patent No 36,836 granted on Tuesday 4 November 1862

The Gatling Gun – the first commercially and practically successful machine gun (*see also 1718*) – was invented during the American Civil War but saw little action in that conflict, partly because Gatling guns were too heavy to be set up quickly; the US government did not officially adopt the Gatling Gun for use by the army until 24 August 1866. It was designed in 1861 (patent granted 1862) by a manufacturer of agricultural machinery named Richard Jordan Gatling, whose previous inventions included a rice planter, a hemp-breaking machine and a steam-plough. Gatling was also a doctor – after enduring smallpox for two weeks without medical treatment aboard an ice-bound river steamer he studied for and passed his medical degree in order to be able to look after his family, although there is no record of him ever practising. His original machine gun had six revolving barrels which were rotated by a hand crank while six cam-operated bolts alternately dropped, wedged and fired the bullets, which were fed by gravity through a hopper mounted on the top of the gun. The reason the gun had six barrels was to allow each one to partially cool during firing – necessary because the original Gatling Gun fired up to 250 rounds per minute, with later, improved versions reaching 1,200 rounds per minute.

❑ ONLY fighting regiment deliberately composed entirely of old men

37th Iowa Volunteer Infantry. American Civil War. Monday 15 December 1862

During the American Civil War the 'Graybeard Regiment' of 914 volunteers was mustered into service for the Union by Captain H B Hendershott of the regular US Army. The regiment, only open to volunteers over the age of 45, included 136 sexagenarians and six septuagenarians, amongst whom was 72-year-old 'drummer-boy' Nicholas Ramey. The oldest man was eighty-year-old Private Curtis King. Although all of them were in good physical condition they were exempt from combat duty and were assigned to guard and garrison duty, their prime function being as a morale booster and a propaganda tool for recruitment. But as it turned out the Graybeards did see direct action. They guarded Confederate rebels in various prisons, provided travelling defence for provisions trains and protected the arsenal at St Louis, which did come under attack. In Holly Springs, Mississippi, the Graybeards engaged a band of rebels and lost several men killed and wounded. In May 1865, with the war almost ended, their commanding officer Brigadier General J Willich requested they be disbanded with honour, adding that although 'Officers and men would cheerfully remain in the service as long as they are wanted ... they are very much needed at home to save the next harvest, most of them being farmers.' The request was granted and on 24 May at Davenport, Iowa, the Graybeards were mustered out of service. The final roll call showed that of a total enrolment of 1,041, three had been killed, 145 had died of disease and 364 had been discharged for wounds, disease or other causes. They may have been old but their courage and sacrifices gave such a glorious example that more than 1,300 sons and grandsons of Graybeard soldiers had enlisted.

❑ ONLY draft-dodging US president

Grover Cleveland. American Civil War. 1863

On 4 March 1885 Grover Cleveland became the 22nd President of the USA. Twenty-two years earlier, while he was assistant district attorney for Erie County, his name had been one of the first drawn in Buffalo under the Conscription Act, which left him in a quandary: apart from the fact he had to support his widowed mother and younger sisters he was a declared anti-war Democrat. There were two options open to him, both legal, if highly unfair: he could buy his way out for $300 under the disguised term 'commutation', or he could find a substitute. Deciding on the latter, cheaper, course he paid a 32-year-old Polish immigrant $150 to take his place as a Union soldier. When this came to light during the 1884 presidential campaign it threatened Cleveland's White House chances – until it was revealed that his Republican opponent James Blaine had done the same thing! Cleveland went on to become the only president to be elected to two non-consecutive terms. Oddly, the anti-war Democrat's nickname for his favourite hunting rifle was 'Death and Destruction'.

☆ FIRST effective attack by submarine

H L Hunley, *Charleston Harbour, South Carolina, USA. American Civil War. Wednesday 17 February 1864*

Confederate submarine *H L Hunley* was made from a steam boiler lengthened by the addition of tapered ends. The tapered ends contained ballast tanks that could be flooded by valves or pumped dry by hand pumps, and extra ballast was provided by iron weights bolted to the hull, which could be released in an emergency by unscrewing the bolts from within the submarine. It was manned by a crew of nine – eight turning a hand-cranked propeller and one steering. Under the command of Lt George Dixon, *H L Hunley* entered Charleston Harbour on 17 February 1864 and sank the Union corvette *Housatonic* by ramming it with a spar torpedo attached to a long pole on its bow. Unfortunately the force of the explosion not only sank *Housatonic*, killing five crew, but also sank *H L Hunley*, killing all nine on board. *H L Hunley* and its sister submarines were nicknamed 'Davids' as they had to battle the 'Goliaths' of the Union Navy.

DID YOU KNOW?

Early in the war Queenie Bennett gave a $20 gold piece to her fiancée George Dixon (*see previous entry*). While he was fighting at Shiloh a Union bullet penetrated Dixon's trouser pocket and struck the gold piece, leaving it shaped like a bell with the bullet embedded in it. If not for that coin the bullet might have prevented Dixon making history on *H L Hunley*. He carried the coin with him for the rest of his life but it didn't bring him luck on the night of his historic attack – the coin was found on board *H L Hunley* when the wreck was discovered in 1995 after a fifteen-year search by bestselling author Clive Cussler.

☆ FIRST meeting of Abraham Lincoln and Ulysses Grant

Abraham Lincoln and General Ulysses Grant, White House, Washington DC. 21:30 Tuesday 8 March 1864

Although President Lincoln had never met General Grant he made him commander-in-chief of the Union forces after Grant had won a series of notable battles. The night before Grant's investiture he travelled to Washington and attended a public reception at the White House. Lincoln shook hands politely with the vast procession of men and women who passed in front of him and then, at about 21:30, there was commotion as Grant approached. Lincoln recognised Grant from pictures he had seen of him and, with a huge smile, advanced towards his distinguished visitor and cried out: 'Why, here is General Grant! Well, this is a great pleasure, I assure you.' Statesman and soldier talked for a few minutes, and then the president presented the general to Secretary of State Seward, who in turn introduced him to the First Lady, Mrs Lincoln. By this time the visitors were so keen to see the famous general that Seward persuaded Grant to stand on a sofa, thinking that would calm everyone down – but instead of satisfying their curiosity this development provoked even more commotion and a rush to shake Grant's hand. The president sent word that he and the secretary of war would await the general in one of the small drawing-rooms, but it was over an hour before Grant was able to make his way there, and then only with the aid of several officers and ushers. The following day Grant returned to the White House to collect his commission and Lincoln invited him to dine there in the evening. But Grant excused himself because he would lose a whole day – and because, he said, 'I have become very tired of this show business.'

DID YOU KNOW?

Lincoln's choice of Grant to lead the Union army was made against Grant's own advice – Grant felt himself not sufficiently competent to command 1,000 soldiers, let alone a complete army. In fact Grant was Lincoln's second choice – Lincoln had already offered the job to Robert E Lee, who is probably the only soldier in history to be offered command of both armies in a war.

✳ LAST words of General John Sedgwick

Battle of Spotsylvania Court House. American Civil War. Monday 9 May 1864

Sedgwick was a hugely popular Union general, known affectionately by his men as 'Uncle John'. During the Battle of Spotsylvania Court House, Confederate sharpshooters were firing from about 1,000 yards, causing Union soldiers and staff to duck for cover. Sedgwick strode around in the open and is quoted as saying: 'What? Men dodging this way for single bullets? What will you do when they open fire along the whole line? I am ashamed of you. They couldn't hit an elephant at this distance.' When his men continued to flinch, he repeated: 'I'm ashamed of you, dodging that way. They couldn't hit an elephant at this dist...' At that moment, he fell forward with a fatal bullet wound below his left eye – or so the story goes. The truth is more prosaic: after Sedgwick's first comment a bullet passed very close and a soldier in front of him dodged to the ground, to which the general said: 'Why, my man, I am ashamed of you, dodging that way. They couldn't hit an elephant at this distance.' The man rose, saluted, and said, 'General, I dodged a shell once, and if I hadn't, it would have taken my head off. I believe in dodging.' The general laughed and replied, 'All right, my man; go to your place.' Those were his actual last words before the fatal bullet hit him, making him the highest-ranking Union casualty of the war – the most senior, by date of rank, of all the major generals killed.

DID YOU KNOW?

A statue of Sedgwick stands in the US Military Academy, and legend has it that cadets who spin Sedgwick's spurs at midnight while wearing full dress uniform will have luck in their exams.

□ **ONLY** bereavement letter sent by Abraham Lincoln to a mother who lost five sons

Abraham Lincoln to Mrs Lydia Bixby. Monday 21 November 1864

> Executive Mansion,
> Washington, Nov. 21, 1864.
>
> Dear Madam,
> I have been shown in the files of the War Department a statement of the Adjutant General of Massachusetts that you are the mother of five sons who have died gloriously on the field of battle.
> I feel how weak and fruitless must be any word of mine which should attempt to beguile you from the grief of a loss so overwhelming. But I cannot refrain from tendering you the consolation that may be found in the thanks of the Republic they died to save.
> I pray that our Heavenly Father may assuage the anguish of your bereavement, and leave you only the cherished memory of the loved and lost, and the solemn pride that must be yours to have laid so costly a sacrifice upon the altar of freedom.
>
> Yours, very sincerely and respectfully,
>
> A. Lincoln

Much later it was revealed that Mrs Bixby was a Confederate sympathiser and brothel keeper who destroyed the letter shortly after receiving it. Only two of her five sons, Charles and Oliver Bixby, had actually died in battle: Sergeant Charles Bixby at the Battle of Fredericksburg in 1862, and Private Oliver Bixby at

Petersburg, Virginia, the following year. Two more sons, Privates George and Edward Bixby, both deserted, and the remaining son, Corporal Henry Bixby, was captured and later swapped in a prisoner exchange. It is also widely believed that the letter was actually written by Lincoln's secretary John Hay.

☆ FIRST person to be judged a war criminal

Captain Henry Wirz, hanged at Old Capitol Prison, Washington, DC. 10:32 Friday 10 November 1865

Swiss-born Confederate Captain Henry Wirz was the commander of the notorious Andersonville Prison in Georgia. Opened in February 1864, it was the largest Confederate prison established during the US Civil War, and during the fourteen months it existed some 45,000 Union soldiers were confined there; 13,171 of them died, many of them teenagers. At its most overcrowded, in August 1864, the camp held approximately 32,000 Union prisoners, making it the fifth largest city in the Confederacy, and the monthly mortality rate from disease and malnutrition reached 3,000. That death toll means that more Union soldiers died in Andersonville than were killed in action in the combined battles of Gettysburg, Antietam, Second Bull Run, Charlottesville, the Wilderness and Appomattox. Wirz boasted he was killing 'more Yankee soldiers than twenty regiments in Lee's army.' The reasons were simple – the compound, enclosing 16.5 acres, was designed to hold 10,000 prisoners, but captives were arriving at a rate of 400 a day. Although the stockade was enlarged by ten acres each man only had about six square feet of living area, much of which was covered in human excrement – it was claimed that the stench of Andersonville could be smelt from a distance of two miles. To make space every tree had been felled, which meant that there was no shelter from the blistering summer heat or sub-zero winter temperatures. A small brook which ran through the camp was used for drinking, washing, cooking and toilets. The meagre and infrequent food rations comprised raw corn meal and maggot-ridden salt bacon. Men were dying of preventable causes such as malnutrition, disease and exposure as well as from the brutality dished out by Wirz, who personally killed prisoners in cold blood and had others hanged, shot, beaten to death, whipped or put in stocks. He also established imaginary 'dead lines' known only to the guards, and had any prisoner found within them to be shot on sight (300 deaths), had escapees hunted down and killed by vicious bloodhounds (50 deaths), and caused 200 deaths and 100 cases of paralysis through experimenting with deadly vaccine injections, harking back to the days when he posed as a doctor. On 7 May 1865, after the Confederate surrender, Wirz was arrested and taken to Washington, DC, to face a federal military tribunal which began on 23 August 1865. The trial was a disgrace, deliberately excluding testimony favourable to Wirz while accepting witness statements describing attacks supposedly made at times when he wasn't even in the camp. After a 63-day trial in which his prime defence was that he was only obeying orders, Wirz was found guilty and sentenced to death. On 10 November 1865 he was taken to the gallows where he thanked Major George B Russell, saying, 'Thank you for your courteous treatment, sir,' before adding, 'I know what your orders are, Major. I am being hanged for obeying them.' Asked if he had any last words, Wirz said, 'I have nothing to say to the public. But to you I say that I am innocent. I can die but once. I have hope for the future.' The black hood was placed over his head and at 10:32 the trapdoor was sprung. But the drop failed to break his neck and Wirz swung round several times with convulsive movements of the legs during the full seven minutes that he took to strangle to death. In 1890 Confederate leader Jefferson Davis wrote a lengthy piece exonerating Wirz, stating: 'He died a martyr to a cause through adherence to truth.'

DID YOU KNOW?

Wirz (*previous entry*) was visited in the death cell by his wife. After she kissed him goodbye officers – suspicious at the sudden display of passion shown by the hitherto restrained couple – grasped Wirz by the throat and ordered him to open his mouth. They found a partly crushed ball, smaller than an acorn, which was found to be a compound of lethal strychnine enclosed in oil silk and coated with liquorice.

❏ **ONLY** VC won for action in Canada
☆ **FIRST** man to win the VC without facing the enemy
☆ **FIRST** VC won in peacetime

Private Timothy O'Hea, 1st Battalion Rifle Brigade, Danville Railway Station, Quebec, Canada. Saturday 9 June 1866

On 9 June 1866 a troop train was carrying the 1st Battalion Rifle Brigade along the Grand Trunk Railway between Quebec and Montreal, Canada. The train was also transporting 800 German immigrants west to the Plains. Irishman O'Hea was detailed to guard a boxcar holding 2,000 pounds of powder and ammunition and in the late afternoon, while at Danville Station, he discovered a fire had broken out and raised the alarm. While everyone else took cover O'Hea disconnected the car carrying the ammunition then snatched the keys to it from the sergeant in charge (who 'was considering what to do') and opened the burning car door. Once inside he tore away the burning material off the covers to the ammunition cases and threw them out of the door. Then, over the next hour, always at risk of being killed, he single-handedly made nineteen trips to a nearby creek to collect water with which to douse the flames. Unaware of the terrible danger, the immigrants cheered him on. He called fellow soldiers to fetch buckets of water which he threw on the flames, finally getting the blaze under control and off-loading the ammunition to another car. His action almost certainly saved not only everyone in the immediate area but also much of the town itself, and he was recommended for the Victoria Cross despite the fact that a provision for winning it is that the action must be in the face of the enemy. By chance that provision was temporarily suspended between 1858–81 and O'Hea deservedly won his medal even though the citation was amended, with classic understatement, to read: 'for conspicuous courage under circumstances of great danger'.

✳ LAST words of the Duke of Valencia

Don Ramón María Narváez y Campos, Duke of Valencia, Madrid, Spain. Thursday 23 April 1868

Don Ramón was a ruthless Spanish soldier and equally ruthless statesman. After a highly successful military career he entered politics and by vicious scheming served repeated terms as prime minister. On his deathbed he was asked if he had forgiven his enemies. His last words were: 'I do not have to forgive my enemies. I have had them all shot.'

☆ FIRST circular battleship
✳ LAST circular battleship

Novgorod, *launched Wednesday 21 May 1873, and* Popov

In 1870 the Russians recognised the need for armoured warships to protect their southern border in the Black Sea, but realised that they would have to be of extremely shallow draught to operate in the Straits of Kerch and the mouth of the Dneiper River. To maximise the weight of armour and armament and minimise the draught, Vice Admiral A A Popov designed a ship whose beam equalled its length – a circular ship. Orders were given to build ten 'Popovki' as floating forts and the first, *Novgorod*, was laid down on 17 December 1871. One hundred and one feet in diameter, *Novgorod* displaced 2,491 tons with, amazingly, a draught of only thirteen feet six inches. But the circular hull increased water resistance so maximum speed was only six knots, achieved by eight coal-fired boilers powering six propellers; the boiler and engine rooms occupied half of the hull which left little living quarters for the 150-man crew. The main deck was convex, with the highest point just five feet three inches above the waterline. This low freeboard made the ship vulnerable in bad weather, exacerbating the fact that the circular design proved unstable: it was almost impossible to keep *Novgorod* steaming in a straight line and it also rolled and pitched excessively even in moderate seas, making accurate gunnery dependent on weather. To make things worse, whenever one of the 26-ton eleven-inch guns was fired the ship would start to spin like a top. Despite all these faults *Novgorod* saw action during the Russo-Turkish War, though she was soon replaced with conventionally-designed ships and ended her days as a store ship at Sevastopol before finally being scrapped in 1912. Although the Russian Admiralty soon realised that the round design was a failure a second, larger 'Popovka' was already nearly built. The world's second and last circular battleship was completed and launched as the *Popov* in honour of its designer – probably the worst designer in naval history.

DID YOU KNOW?

Popov was not the first to advocate a circular ship. Sir Edward Reed, chief designer for the Royal Navy in late 1860s, had considered circular ships for British coastal defence but they were never built.

❑ ONLY survivor of Custer's Last Stand
✳ LAST major battle by Native Americans

Comanche, Battle of the Little Big Horn, lower valley of the Little Big Horn River, Montana. 25-26 June 1876

Comanche was a 15-hand bay gelding, thought to be part-mustang and part-Morgan. Bought by the US Army in 1868, he was such a handsome horse that instead of allowing him to be kept with the regular cavalry horses, Captain Myles Keogh, a member of Custer's 7th Cavalry, bought him for $90 to use as his personal mount. In autumn 1868 Comanche was injured in Kansas – ironically, while fighting the Comanche tribe. Unaware of his horse's injury, Keogh continued to fight from his back until the battle was over, and only later did he discover an arrow broken off in Comanche's hindquarters. In 1870 Comanche was wounded in the leg, and a year after that he was wounded in the shoulder. In 1876 Keogh rode Comanche into the valley of the Little Big Horn to fight what would be the Native Americans' last great battle – they massacred the US cavalry, including every soldier who supported Custer in his famous last stand. The only member of the 7th Cavalry left alive after the battle was Comanche, who was found two days later, weakened by his many wounds and barely able to stand. Supported by a sling, he was taken by steamboat to Fort Lincoln, where he was nursed back to health and officially retired with the title 'Second Commanding Officer of the 7th Cavalry' and orders that no one would ever ride him again. He occasionally took the place of honour leading official parades and was, understandably, spoiled by admirers who delighted in indulging Comanche's passion for beer. He died at the ripe old age of 29, after which his body was preserved; it is still on display at the University of Kansas.

✻ LAST of the Samurai

Battle of Shiroyama, near Tahara-zaka hill in Kagoshima, Japan.
Monday 24 September 1877

Saigo Takamori was a Japanese Samurai soldier and statesman whose politics were popular with traditionalists. However, his ultra-conservative stance eventually led to his deposition, after which he opened a military school in his native Kagoshima, attracting disaffected former Samurai. He spent four years training a military force and, in 1877, led the six-month Satsuma Revolt against the central government, culminating in a last stand at the Battle of Shiroyama. It was a hopeless situation – although the Imperial troops were mainly conscripts there were 300,000 of them, equipped with rifles, cannon, Gatling Guns and observation balloons. Saigo's tiny army of 300-400 elderly Samurai was all that remained of his original 25,000-strong force. Undaunted by the odds, Saigo's men charged the Imperial lines and the conscripts were soon in disarray, being no match for the Samurai in close-quarter sword fighting. But the lesson was learned, and before the Samurai could organise a second charge they were mown down from a safe distance by Imperial cannon and Gatling Gun fire. Saigo was hit with a near-fatal shot to his femoral artery, and in order to prevent himself being killed or captured he committed seppuku (hara-kiri) by plunging his sword into his stomach and disembowelling himself before being decapitated by a fellow Samurai. His head, hidden by a comrade, was never found, prompting many legends that Saigo was still alive and plotting the return of the Samurai – but in fact his suicide marked the end of the Samurai. To avoid another rebellion, and as a mark of respect to the courage of the Samurai, Emperor Meiji granted Saigo a posthumous pardon on 22 February 1889. Saigo's last stand inspired the final scenes of the feature film, *The Last Samurai*.

☆ FIRST British general immortalised in an operetta

Field Marshal Sir Garnet Wolseley, as Major General Stanley in The Pirates of Penzance, *Paignton, Devon. Tuesday 30 December 1879*

Wolseley was the inspiration for Major General Stanley, 'The Modern Major General', in Gilbert and Sullivan's operetta *The Pirates of Penzance*. His career got off to a poor start when he was seriously wounded in Burma and then again in the Crimea, where one side of his face was completely cut open – before sewing back his cheek one doctor had to grip Wolseley's head between his knees while another tugged a stone splinter out of his jaw. This terrible injury resulted in the loss of an eye but that didn't stop Wolseley serving with distinction in India, China, Canada and Africa. He claimed that he tried to get killed every time he had a chance, and that 'man-shooting is the finest sport of all ... the more you kill them more you wish to kill.' Ironically, he couldn't bear the sight of raw meat or pass a butcher's shop without feeling ill. His amazing military exploits made him a household name, and when *The Pirates of Penzance* was first performed in Paignton, Devon on 30 December 1879, actor George Goldsmith was made up to look like Wolseley. With typical enthusiasm Wolseley was thrilled at the caricature and subsequently delighted in entertaining his friends by singing:

> I am the very model of a modern Major General
> I've information vegetable, animal and mineral ...

DID YOU KNOW?

During the Peninsular War, when one of his officers asked for extended leave, Wolseley refused, saying, 'Forty-eight hours in bed with a woman is enough.'

❏ ONLY combat animal to be decorated by a reigning monarch

Bobbie, Osborne House, Isle of Wight. Wednesday 17 August 1881

The Battle of Maiwand, fought on 27 July 1880, was one of the largest battles of the Second Anglo-Afghan War and one of the few nineteenth-century battles in which an Asiatic power defeated a western one. The 2,566 British were outnumbered ten to one by the 25,000 Afghans but the 66th Regiment of Foot fought a heroic last stand during which the last eleven men, when ammunition was exhausted, charged with the bayonet to their deaths. The only survivor of the massacre of the 66th was their mascot, a white white-haired mongrel bitch named Bobbie, who barked defiantly at the enemy throughout the slaughter. The 66th's self-sacrificial last stand made it possible for the British survivors, including the wounded Bobbie, to retreat to Kandahar. After returning to England Bobbie, wearing a scarlet coat trimmed with fake pearls, was presented to Queen Victoria at Osborne House. When told of Bobbie's remarkable career Victoria asked to see her war wound and then ceremoniously pinned the Afghan War campaign medal on Bobbie's smart new collar. A year later, on 13 October 1882, Bobbie was accidentally killed by a hansom cab in Gosport. On hearing the news the Queen is said to have cried.

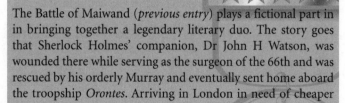

DID YOU KNOW?

The Battle of Maiwand (*previous entry*) plays a fictional part in in bringing together a legendary literary duo. The story goes that Sherlock Holmes' companion, Dr John H Watson, was wounded there while serving as the surgeon of the 66th and was rescued by his orderly Murray and eventually sent home aboard the troopship *Orontes*. Arriving in London in need of cheaper lodgings, he met his old dresser Stamford at St Batholomew's Hospital, at the Criterion Bar. Stamford suggested that Watson meet an acquaintance named Sherlock Holmes, and the two went on to share rooms at 221B Baker Street.

❑ ONLY travel agency to organise transport to take an army to war

Thomas Cook & Son. Wednesday 28 January 1885

From 18 March 1884 General Charles Gordon, defending a garrison of 8,000 Egyptian and loyal Sudanese troops at Khartoum, was besieged by 50,000 followers of the Mahdi Muhammad Ahmad. The British government had decided to abandon the Sudan but it was clear that Gordon had other plans, and the public insisted that the government support him. Finally, in November, the government decided to send a force to relieve Gordon. The British War Office requested Thomas Cook & Son to make the travel arrangements. With remarkable efficiency and speed Cook's arranged 27 steamships, 28 ocean liners, 650 sailboats and 800 whaleboats to transport 18,000 troops and 130,000 tons of ammunition to the Sudan. Despite overwhelming odds the troops arrived precisely on schedule on 28 January 1885. To their horror they found that just two days earlier the city had been captured and the entire garrison killed.

DID YOU KNOW?

In 1841 Thomas Cook began organising railway excursions to Temperance Society meetings, thereby establishing the world's earliest surviving travel agency. In 1862 he organised the first package holiday and by the late nineteenth century tourists were often referred to as 'Cookii' or 'il Cucchi'.

☆ FIRST use of the Digger Hat by Australian troops

Victorian Mounted Rifles. Thursday 3 December 1885

The symbol of the Australian army – the Digger Hat, or Slouch Hat, with one side of the brim turned up – first became part of an Australian military uniform on 3 December 1885, when it was chosen for the newly-formed Victorian Mounted Rifles by the commanding officer, Colonel Tom Price. It was made from rabbit-fur felt or wool felt, with a leather chin strap and the distinctive turn-up on the right side. There are two schools of thought as to the purpose of the turn-up: first, that it was to keep the brim out of the way of a lance held in a stirrup cup or of a rifle-and-bayonet carried over the shoulder; or, second, that it was to make it easier for marching troops to perform the 'eyes right' command in parades. Years later, F D Price – the originator's youngest son, a former member of the unit and a veteran of the Boer War – related the origin of the hat to his father's experience in Burma, where native police wore similar head-dress. The Burmese hat included a two-piece buckled chinstrap and a prominent three-plait of puggaree – puggaree being a traditional Indian head-wrap designed to keep the head cool, and adapted by the British for hot, sunny regions. The Slouch Hat made its first appearance overseas on the heads of Australian troops fighting in the Boer War, and it added much to their mystique. The most striking innovation was the addition of the plumes of various birds, including black cock, eagle, swan, ostrich and, most famously of all, emu. It is believed that emu plumage was first adopted by the Queensland Mounted Infantry who, to prove their horsemanship, were required to ride alongside an emu running at full speed and pluck its darker and smaller chest feathers – it was a matter of honour to pluck the feathers from a running bird, and taking feathers from a dead bird was not acceptable.

DID YOU KNOW?

Contrary to popular belief the word 'slouch' (*previous entry*) does not refer to the turn-up, or leaf – it refers to any hat with a brim that droops down. Also, Australians did not 'invent' the turned-up brim on a slouch hat; it was worn like that by many armies, with and without feathers, over hundreds of years. But the Diggers made it famous, and it is now it is recognised as an exclusively Australian trademark – just don't tell the Gurkhas.

＊ LAST time British infantry wore scarlet tunics in battle

Battle of Ginniss, Sudan, Africa. First Sudan War. 10:00 Thursday 31 December 1885

The last occasion that British infantry wore the traditional scarlet tunic in action was at the Battle of Ginniss, in which General Stephenson launched a dawn attack on the Dervishes at Ginniss, on the banks of the Nile in Egyptian-held Sudan. By 10:00 the Dervishes had repulsed the attack, liberating Sudan and marking the end both of the First Sudan War and of the red coat.

❑ ONLY war to last thirty-eight minutes

Battle of Zanzibar, Zanzibar (now part of Tanzania), Africa. 09:02-09:40 Thursday 27 August 1896

Zanzibar became a British protectorate in 1890. The death of Sultan Hamad bin Thuwaini on 25 August 1896 saw his nephew Seyyid Khalid bin Bargash usurp the throne from Sultan Hamoud bin Mohammed, whom the British considered the rightful ruler. The British therefore demanded that Bargash relinquish his title.

Two days later, at 07:00, he was given a final two-hour ultimatum – abdication or war. Bargash had already decided on war, and had fortified his palace and organised his army of 2,800 to face the might of the British Empire; he had also armed the former sultan's yacht, an aged wooden-hulled steam frigate named *Glasgow*, which the British had sold to bin Thuwani instead of selling for scrap. The Royal Navy assembled three cruisers and two gunboats in the harbour in front of the palace, and landed parties of Royal Marines to support the 'loyalist' regular army of Zanzibar. With no reply forthcoming from the Sultan, the Anglo-Zanzibar War began at 09:02. The British ships bombarded the palace, reducing it to rubble, while the Zanzibar Navy (ie, the *Glasgow*) was quickly blasted out of the water. A ceasefire was declared at 09:40, by which time Khalid had fled to the German Consulate, where he was granted asylum. The British demanded that the Germans surrender Bargash, but he escaped and lived in exile in Dar es Salaam until captured by the British in 1916. He was later allowed to live in Mombasa where he died in 1927. Sultan Hamoud was declared the new ruler and, agreeing to British demands, banned slavery – he freed and compensated all slaves in Zanzibar and also agreed to pay the British Government for the shells fired on his country.

❑ ONLY British prime minister to have escaped from a prisoner of war camp

Winston Churchill, State Model School Prisoner of War Camp, Pretoria, South Africa. Boer War. 18:55 Tuesday 12 December 1899

As a 24-year-old journalist, Churchill was dispatched to South Africa to cover the Boer War for the *London Morning Post*. Anxious to witness the action at first hand, he accompanied an armoured train on a reconnaissance mission into enemy-held

Natal, and on 15 November 1899 the train was ambushed. After organising an attempt to free the locomotive Churchill tried to escape up an embankment but lost his revolver in the process, so when a Boer soldier armed with a rifle rode towards him, Churchill surrendered. He was interned in the State Model School POW camp despite complaining that, as a civilian non-combatant, he was being held unjustly, and he soon began making an escape plan with Captain Aylmer Haldane and Sergeant-Major Brockie. On 12 December, after abortive attempts earlier that night and the night before, Churchill strolled over to the latrine which abutted the camp perimeter, and as the sentry turned to light his pipe Churchill jumped on to a ledge, climbed the ten-foot wall and dropped into a garden on the other side. For more than ninety minutes he hid behind a bush waiting for Brockie and Haldane, while twice a man from the house walked along a path within seven or eight yards of him. Eventually Churchill heard a fellow soldier using the toilet and whispered through the wall that Haldane and Brockie must make their move immediately. Haldane returned to the latrine but was spotted, so Churchill decided he must make his escape alone. With sheer bravado, and making no attempt at concealment, he calmly walked straight out of the garden gate in the glare of an electric light, passing a guard who stood only nine feet away. He then strolled through the suburbs of Pretoria, where no one challenged him, but his greatest challenge lay ahead – he faced 300 miles of hostile Boer territory to make safety at Delagoa Bay in neutral Portuguese East Africa. He had no compass, no map, no local knowledge, and didn't speak Dutch or the local dialect (Xhosa). But he did have a plan: his only hope was to risk boarding the nightly train to Delagoa Bay. He found the railway track and followed it, skirting round the camp fires of sentries guarding the line, and after two hours he saw the lights of the station. He hid in a ditch nearby, planning to leap aboard before the train had gathered speed, on an uphill outward curve where he would be hidden from both the driver and the guard. At the third attempt he managed to swing himself aboard, and slept on a pile of coal sacks. At dawn, fearing discovery, he leapt off the train and headed east. Meanwhile, a reward of £25 had been issued for his capture, dead or alive. He was described as being 'About five foot eight or nine inches, blonde with light thin small moustache, walks with a slight stoop, cannot speak any Dutch, during long conversations he occasionally makes a rattling noise in his throat.' Churchill was completely lost on the veldt but at last he spotted a light and, with little option, tentatively approached. At 01:30 his knock was answered by John Howard, holding a revolver. Churchill told him: 'I am Dr Bentick. I have fallen off the train.' Howard covered him with his gun, believing him to be a Boer spy, but at last Churchill made a clean breast of it at which point Howard locked the door, shook his hand, and said, 'Thank God you have come here! It is the only house for twenty miles where you would not have been handed over. We are all British here and we will see you through.' After feeding him, Howard hid Churchill at the bottom of a mine and provided him with candles, whisky and a box of cigars, but when Churchill awoke he discovered that rats had eaten the candles. He spent three days underground, until 02:00 on the 19 December, when Howard led him to a railway wagon where he was hidden among bales of wool. When the train reached Ressano Garcia, the first station in Portuguese East Africa, Churchill surfaced from his woolly hideout and, he recalls, 'sang and shouted and crowed at the top of my voice.'

DID YOU KNOW?

The mounted Boer soldier who captured Churchill was Louis Botha, who was destined to become the first Prime Minister of South Africa and a firm and loyal friend of Britain.

✽ LAST surviving veteran of the War of 1812

Hiram Cronk. Saturday 13 May 1905

Cronk, born in Frankport, New York, on 29 April 1800, was the last surviving veteran of the War of 1812 when he died on 13 May 1905 at the age of 105. On 14 August 1814 he and his father and two brothers enlisted with the New York Volunteers. After seeing action in the defence of Sackett's Harbor, Cronk was discharged on 16 November 1814 became a cobbler for the remainder of his life, and at the time of his death he had fourteen grandchildren and eight great-grandchildren. Financially, his 104 days of military service proved quite rewarding: he received an automatic pension of $12 per month, which in 1903 Congress increased to $25 per month, and he also received a special pension of $72 per month from the State of New York – a total of well over $40,000, or nearly $400 per day of service. When he died, his body was displayed in the main lobby of New York City Hall, where an estimated 25,000 people paid their respects.

✽ LAST American Civil War veteran to die as a result of wounds sustained during the war

Joshua Lawrence Chamberlain. Tuesday 24 February 1914

Chamberlain was an outstanding academic who, without any formal military education, became a highly-respected and highly-decorated Union general during the American Civil War. He took part in 24 engagements during which he was wounded six times and had six horses shot from under him. In a major action at Rives' Salient on 18 June 1863, Chamberlain was shot through the right hip and groin and, in order to stay upright and not to dishearten his men, stuck his sword in the ground and leaned on it for some time before falling unconscious. Two surgeons operated but considered he had little hope of surviving, and General Grant gave him a battlefield promotion to brigadier general. Incredibly he survived and was back in command within five months. Grant gave him the honour of commanding the Union troops at the eventual surrender of Robert E Lee's infantry, where his gallant conduct and respect for the defeated Confederates earned him the approbation of many Northerners – but a greater number considered him the 'knightliest' soldier in the Federal Army. After the war Chamberlain served as a Republican Governor of Maine for four terms but he carried a permanent reminder of his military career: for the remainder of his long life he had to wear a silver catheter in his abdomen with a bag to drain a wound that never healed. Despite six operations the wound persistently caused severe fevers and major infections. Chamberlain died as a direct result of his wartime wounds on 24 February 1914 at Portland, Maine, at the age of 85. At his deathbed he was attended by Dr Abner Shaw, one of the two surgeons who had operated on him in Petersburg half a century earlier.

☆ FIRST British soldier to fire on the enemy in the First World War

Corporal Thomas, C Squadron, 4th Irish Dragoons, near Soignes, France. First World War. Saturday 22 August 1914

The British Expeditionary Force arrived in France in 1914 to face its first military engagement in Western Europe since the Battle of Waterloo 99 years earlier. Kaiser Wilhelm II denounced the BEF as a 'contemptible little army' but they turned his insult into a badge of honour by dubbing themselves the 'Old Contemptibles'. Just after dawn on 22 August, while patrolling the road from Masieres,

Corporal Thomas spotted the German cavalrymen of the 2nd Kuirassiers and became the first British soldier of the First World War to open fire against the enemy. C Squadron pursued the enemy and their commander returned with a bloodied sword and three wounded enemy prisoners, all of whom had suffered sword cuts. It was clear that the new war was going to be fought just like Waterloo – or so they thought.

❏ ONLY army saved by a fleet of taxi cabs

Battle of the Marne, Marne River near Paris, France. First World War. Monday 7 September 1914

During the First Battle of the Marne (5 September to 12 September 1914) the German forces were close to achieving a critical breakthrough against the 6th Army defending Paris. Trains carrying relief infantrymen of the 103rd and 104th regiments were delayed by France's choked railway system, and on 6 September 1914 General Joseph-Simon Gallieni, the military governor of Paris, suggested they travel by road instead. When told there was an acute shortage of army motor vehicles and drivers, Gallieni said: 'Why not use taxis?' All Parisian taxis and their drivers were immediately assembled at the Esplanade des Invalides and all agreed to help, despite one truly Gallic driver demanding: 'What about the fare?' The lead column of about 150 empty taxis left Paris that night, and at 04:00 on 7 September the convoy, now grown to an estimated 600 taxis plus uncounted stray trucks, limousines and racing cars, arrived at a railway siding to load the reinforcements. Each trip brought five soldiers close to the front ready for deployment and most of the cabs were sent back to take a second load, so by 8 September the taxis of the Marne had transported about 4,000 badly needed soldiers to reinforce the 6th Army facing the Germans near

Nanteuil. With these reinforcements the 6th Army won a vital victory; Paris was saved and the Taxi Cabs of the Marne became a national legend. And the fare? The drivers eventually received 27 per cent of the meter reading.

❏ ONLY man to win the VC and an Olympic gold medal

Lieutenant (later Lieutenant General) Philip Neame (later Sir Philip Neame). Thursday 19 November 1914

On 18 November 1914, British infantry captured the German trenches at Neuve Chapelle. The next morning the Germans counter-attacked and Neame (nephew of one of the founders of the Kent brewery Shepherd Neame) was ordered to help consolidate the British position with trenches and wiring. Advancing alone to reconnoitre, Neame discovered, in a forward trench, the remnants of the West Yorkshire Regiment's bombing squad under attack from German bombers. The West Yorkshires' sergeant held out a sandbag filled with improvised jam-tin bombs and said, 'Why don't you try some of these bombs, Sir?' Neame trimmed the damp fuses and began hurling them over the trenches at the Germans, and every time he stood to launch another bomb he was fired on by a machine gun. Despite twice being grazed in the neck by bullets he single-handedly repulsed the Germans for over an hour, then assisted the wounded to safety. For his outstanding courage he was awarded the VC. Neame was a noted marksman, and in 1924 he competed as part of the British sporting rifle team at the Paris Olympics. He won a gold in the now-discontinued sport of Team Running Deer Shooting (single shot), in which a moving target simulated the animal. He had honed his skills in Europe and South Asia, indulging in his 'great passion' – killing big game, especially tigers and panthers.

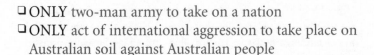

❏ **ONLY** two-man army to take on a nation
❏ **ONLY** act of international aggression to take place on Australian soil against Australian people

Battle of Broken Hill, New South Wales, Australia. Friday 1 January 1915

History's smallest army was formed on New Year's Eve, 1914, and within 24 hours it had been annihilated. The army consisted of sixty-year-old butcher Mulla Abdullah and ice cream vendor Gool Mahomet; their entire armour was two rifles, and their transport was a multi-coloured ice cream cart. In October 1914 the Sultan of Turkey declared jihad (holy war) against the British Empire and when Abdullah and Mahomet, two Muslim immigrants residing in the tiny outback mining town of Broken Hill, heard about the jihad on New Year's Eve they decided it was their religious duty to take action. The next day hundreds of excited locals clambered aboard railway trucks for the trip to Silverton for the annual New Year's Day Miners' Picnic. Three miles out of Broken Hill Abdullah and Mahomet opened fire from behind the ice cream cart, which flew a Turkish flag they had made from a tablecloth. They fired twenty or thirty shots, killing four people and wounding six others, including fifteen-year-old Lucy Shaw. They then fled to White Rocksmiles, where police and militia surrounded their stone barricade in a six-hour stand-off. Rejecting calls to surrender, Abdullah and Mahomet chanted patriotic songs until finally they both died in a fusillade of bullets. An angry mob then descended on the local Afghan Mosque (actually a small tin shack), where Abdullah had acted as imam, and attacked many innocent Muslims before the militia was able to disperse the frenzied crowd. It later transpired that both men knew they would die and had left notes stating that they were dying for their faith and in obedience to the order of the sultan. The Battle of Broken Hill resulted in Attorney General

Billy Hughes ordering that all enemy aliens in Australia be interned for the duration of the war. Oddly, although Abdullah and Mahomet flew the Turkish flag and caused great animosity towards Turks, the two-man army actually came from Afghanistan.

☆ FIRST air raid fatalities in Britain

Samuel Smith and Martha Taylor, St Peter's Plain, Great Yarmouth, Norfolk. First World War. 20:30 Tuesday 19 January 1915

The historic first casualties were killed by the German Zeppelin *L3*, which dropped six 110-pound bombs and a number of incendiaries over Great Yarmouth, a seaside town with little military significance. The first bomb fell 'in a meadow at Ormesby' just before 20:25 and the second destroyed a stable at the rear of 78 Crown Road. Fifty-three-year-old cobbler Sam Smith heard the explosions and came out of his workshop in St Peter's Plain to see what was happening. At 20:30 the third bomb hit a house opposite and he was killed instantly by flying shrapnel. At the same moment 72-year-old spinster Martha Taylor was killed 'as she was going for her supper'. Three others were injured. Meanwhile *L3*'s sister airship, *L2*, went further inland and bombed King's Lynn, another town with no military significance, killing two civilians and injuring thirteen. The cost of the damage was estimated at £7,740.

DID YOU KNOW?

In total, British casualties from air raids carried out by airships were 1,914, with 556 killed; those from raids carried out by aeroplanes were 2,908 with 857 killed – a total of 4,822 casualties with 1,413 killed.

❑ ONLY British woman to have officially fought in the First World War

Flora Sandes. First World War. Monday 22 November 1915

When war broke out in August 1914, 38-year-old Sandes immediately volunteered as a Volunteer Aid Detachment nurse. She was rejected, but subsequently invited to join the Red Cross. She travelled with six other volunteer nurses to a military hospital in Kragujev, Serbia, where they tended over 1,000 injured men with only basic equipment, and with anaesthetics reserved for only the worst cases. After four months Sandes embarked on a fund-raising mission to England, returning six weeks later with 120 tons of medicine and equipment. She then volunteered to go to Valjevo, where 200 people a day were dying of typhus and 21 doctors had died in three weeks, leaving just one doctor to treat the sick. Sandes caught typhus but survived, and with no option she took on the role of doctor, on one occasion amputating a man's toes with a pair of scissors because she had no other equipment. Again she returned to England to raise funds, and on her return to the war zone she was attached to the Ambulance of the Second Infantry Regiment in Southern Macedonia. But she soon found a more aggressive role for herself, writing, 'I seem to have just drifted, by successive stages, from a nurse into a soldier.' Because she had proved herself brave and fearless, and could shoot, ride, drive and speak four languages, she was formally inducted into the Serbian army as a private on 22 November 1915. Almost a year later, on 15 November 1916, as the Serbians attacked Monastir, a Bulgar hand-bomb knocked Sandes unconscious, smashed her arm and caused over a dozen wounds on her back and side. Comrades dragged her off the battlefield just in time – when they returned to continue fighting they found twelve members of her unit laid out in a neat row with their throats cut. While in hospital Sandes was awarded Serbia's highest military honour, the Kara George Star, and after being discharged, though permanently disabled, she returned to the front line with 'half a blacksmith's shop' still embedded in her. Promoted sergeant and then captain, she remained in the Serbian army until 1921. But that wasn't the end of her military career – at the age of 64, despite her disabilities, she was called up to serve in the Second World War. She was captured by the Germans and taken to a military prison hospital, but escaped after donning women's civilian clothes and strolling out of the jail. After the war she retired to Suffolk, where she died from obstructive jaundice on 24 November 1956. The only British woman to have fought officially in the First World War said, 'Turning from a woman to a private soldier was nothing compared with turning back from soldier to ordinary woman.'

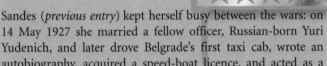

DID YOU KNOW?

Sandes (*previous entry*) kept herself busy between the wars: on 14 May 1927 she married a fellow officer, Russian-born Yuri Yudenich, and later drove Belgrade's first taxi cab, wrote an autobiography, acquired a speed-boat licence, and acted as a matron at the Folies Bergères in Paris. Returning to Belgrade, she acted for the Serbs as a fund-raiser and unofficial ambassador.

❏ **ONLY** dead soldier to become a national leader

Charles de Gaulle. Thursday 2 March 1916

After passing out of Saint-Cyr military academy (the French equivalent of West Point or Sandhurst) in 1912, de Gaulle decided to join an infantry regiment rather than an elite corps. At 13:15 on 2 March 1916, between La Calvaire and Douaumont church, the

Germans launched an advance on the isolated 10th Company of the 3rd Battalion, under the command of Captain de Gaulle. At first the French didn't fire, thinking the attackers were comrades until they were close enough to be identified as Germans wearing French helmets. Then the French, with de Gaulle at their head, courageously charged the enemy and fought a series of fierce hand-to-hand struggles. Such was the carnage that it was assumed de Gaulle had been killed with his men, and for his astonishing bravery he was posthumously awarded the Croix de Chevalier de la Legion d'Honneur. In fact, having flung a hand grenade, he had leapt into a shell hole at the same time as several Germans, one of whom bayoneted him. The blade passed diagonally through de Gaulle's left thigh, the unbearable pain causing him to pass out, and when he came to was taken first to a hospital in Mainz and then to a transit camp at Neisse. He remained a prisoner of war for thirty months, until the end of the First World War, during which time he made at least five major escape attempts – however, his conspicuous height betrayed him every time.

DID YOU KNOW?

Because of his height the other cadets at Saint-Cyr military academy nicknamed de Gaulle 'The Long Asparagus'.

☆ FIRST battle with more than one million casualties

First Battle of the Somme, France, between the Somme and Ancre Rivers from Chaulnes in the south to Beaumont-Hamel in the north. First World War. 07:20 Saturday 1 July 1916

The bloodiest day in the history of the British army began at 07:20, ten minutes before the Battle of the Somme was planned to begin, when a British officer, for reasons unknown, detonated a

21-ton mine beneath the Hawthorn Ridge Redoubt, obliterating the German garrison above. Eight minutes later eight of the remaining nine mines exploded, and at 07:30 the whistles blew and the British soldiers climbed out of their trenches into the jaws of hell. The British believed the Germans had been softened by a five-day bombardment of 1,732,873 shells (the explosions were heard on Hampstead Heath in London) but in fact they had been safely entrenched in secret bunkers thirty to forty feet below ground. The British were convinced that all they had to do was walk in and take over; neither were they afraid of machine guns because, according to Field Marshal Lord Douglas Haig, 'The machine gun is an over-rated weapon.' One of his brigadier generals was even more blasé, telling his men: 'You'll be able to go over the top with just a walking stick – you won't need rifles ... You'll find the Germans all dead; not even a rat will have survived.' Such was the British confidence that some officers just carried their swagger sticks, one armed himself with only his umbrella and another kicked a rugby ball for his men to chase. The slaughter was unimaginable. The British lumbered forward, struggling to free themselves from the uncut barbed wire, straight toward the German guns. Wave after wave of Tommies advancing two yards apart in successive ranks 100 yards behind each other were wasted by German machine guns. On the first day British losses were 19,240 killed, 35,493 wounded, 2,152 missing (presumably blown to pieces) and 585 captured: a total of 57,470 – the highest casualty rate and the worst death toll for a single day in the history of the British army. And that was just the first day – the battle raged until 19 November, becoming the bloodiest single modern battle with casualties recorded at 1,043,896, comprising 623,907 Allied soldiers (419,654 of them British) and the rest German. The British lost 2,943 men per day and ultimately gained approximately two miles of ground. Each centimetre cost the lives of two men.

☆ FIRST airship brought down over England
☆ FIRST man to win a VC in (actually, over) the UK

Lieutenant W Leefe Robinson, 39 Squadron RFC, Cuffley, Hertfordshire. First World War. 02:05 Sunday 3 September 1916

The largest single airship raid of the First World War began on the night of 2/3 September 1916, when sixteen German airships targeted London. Just after 02:00, as airship *SL11* began bombing Edmonton and Ponders End, it came under attack from a BE 2c twin-seater reconnaissance aircraft from 39 Squadron, piloted by 21-year-old Lieutenant William Leefe Robinson. After a diving attack, Leefe Robinson raked the hull of *SL11* from beneath with new explosive bullets filled with nitro-glycerine, which were designed to ignite the hydrogen filling the airship, but to no avail. He made a second run and emptied another drum of bullets along the flank of *SL11*, again with no apparent damage. With only one drum of bullets left he flew to within 500 feet of the airship's belly and aimed for a single section of her hull. Before the drum was empty *SL11* began to glow, and within seconds the rear part of the hull erupted in flames. Leefe Robinson was forced to take immediate evasive action to avoid being dragged to earth by the plummeting airship, which crashed in a field behind the Plough Inn at Cuffley, killing all sixteen crew members. With hardly any fuel left Leefe Robinson headed straight back to Sutton's Farm aerodrome (which would play a pivotal role in the Battle of Britain during the Second World War, under its new name of Hornchurch) where he landed at 02:45. He subsequently discovered that part of his central top wing and machine gun wire had been shot away, which meant that he had been in constant danger of the plane breaking up in midair. Thousands of Londoners witnessed *SL11*'s last moments, and Leefe Robinson woke to find himself a hero – 10,000 people visited the crash site and babies, flowers and even hats were named after him. His VC was announced within 48 hours and the presentation was made by George V at Windsor Castle three days later – the same day that *SL11*'s sixteen crew-members were buried. Leefe Robinson was modest about his triumph, saying, 'I only did my job.' Embarrassed by the public adulation, he requested a posting to France where, on 5 April 1917, while leading six planes of 48 Squadron on his first operational sortie, he was attacked by the Red Baron, Manfred von Richthofen, and four of his veteran fighter pilots. Four of the British planes were shot down, while Leefe Robinson was forced to land and was taken prisoner. His reputation preceded him and he was treated brutally by his captors. After each of four escape attempts his treatment grew worse, until eventually fellow prisoners made a full report of the way he was being brutalised, smuggled it out of the camp in a hollow tennis racket handle, and somehow managed to get it delivered to the War Office. After the armistice Leefe Robinson eventually arrived home on 14 December 1918. He died seventeen days later on New Year's Eve, officially from heart failure brought on by influenza, but there can be little doubt he died as a result of the cruelty he suffered as a prisoner of war. He was twenty-three.

DID YOU KNOW?

SL11 was actually a wooden-framed airship not, as is often assumed, a Zeppelin. Its captain, Commander Wilhelm Schramm, was born in London and died just a few miles from his birthplace. The Zeppelin, which had a rigid skin rather than a skeleton, was invented by Count Ferdinand Graf Zeppelin, who filed a patent on 31 August 1895 for a 'navigable balloon'. In 1908 Zeppelin used a fleet of airships to establish Delag as the world's first commercial airline, and when the First World War broke out he urged the use of airships to bomb Britain.

☆ FIRST tank in battle
☆ FIRST tank casualties
☆ FIRST tank to be disabled by the enemy

Tank DI, Battle of Flers-Courcelette, Somme, France. First World War. 06:00 Friday 15 September 1916

A new epoch in land warfare began during the Battle of Flers-Courcelette, with the debut of the tank. In 1915, after continued pressure from Winston Churchill, the War Office produced a specification for an armoured bullet-proof vehicle that could cross a 1.7metre ditch and climb a 1.7metre bank. The prototypes, called 'Little Willie' and 'Mother', were produced in Lincoln, and mass production began in February 1916. Finally 'Mother' was ready. Thirty-three feet long, weighing 28 tons, and with a top speed of 4mph, she carried a crew of eight and was armed with two machine guns and two six-pounder cannon in 'sponsons' – armoured boxes on either side of her hull which, to preserve secrecy, were referred to as 'tanks' from their resemblance to large water tanks. The British had high hopes that this secret weapon would break the deadlock of trench warfare, though some had reservations – including an aide-de-camp to Field Marshal Douglas Haig, who said, 'The idea that cavalry will be replaced by these iron coaches is absurd. It is little short of treasonous.' Haig himself was impressed enough to want 100 tanks but they proved notoriously unreliable: of the 49 available on 15 September, only 32 made it to the start line, and of these only 21 made it into action. Just after 06:00 tank DI, commanded by Captain W H Mortimore, went into action alongside another tank, successfully breaking though German lines and reaching the village of Flers. Haig was thrilled, and excitedly told waiting pressmen the great news. What he didn't mention was that one of the tanks had lost its bearings and accidentally machine-gunned a trench sheltering members of the 9th Norfolks, killing dozens of British soldiers and leaving the Germans unharmed. With cruel irony, when the survivors of the 9th Norfolks attacked later they were massacred by the very German defenders who had been the tank's real target. Meanwhile Mortimore, after taking German prisoners, received a direct hit on his starboard sponson which resulted in the deaths of two of the crew, who thus became the world's first tank casualties. The fire also destroyed Mortimore's track, making DI not only the first tank into action but also the first to be taken out of action by the enemy. However, although tanks were mechanically unreliable, underpowered, dangerously slow and vulnerable to becoming bogged down, their success was out of proportion to the numbers employed – they were here to stay.

✱ LAST words of Saki

Hector Hugh Munro, aka Saki, Beaumont-Hamel, Battle of Ancre, France. First World War. Tuesday 14 November 1916

Munro was a master author whose short stories invariably had a sting in the tale. He wrote under the pseudonym Saki, the name of the 'cypress-slender Minister of Wine' in the Rubáiyát of Omar Khayyám. In August 1914 the 44-year-old writer enlisted in the ranks, refusing a commission and preferring to serve as a corporal and eventually a lance sergeant. Although suffering from malaria, he discharged himself from hospital on 11 November 1916 when he heard an offensive was due. He was killed by a sniper's bullet three days later, during the final assault on Beaumont Hamel during the battle of Ancre. Knowing that the first strike of a light would attract a sniper's attention, the second confirm the sighting and the third give the sniper a target, Munro's last words were a prophetic admonishment to one of his men: 'Put that bloody cigarette out!'

☆ FIRST landing of a plane on a ship under way

Squadron Commander E H Dunning, HMS Furious. *First World War. Thursday 2 August 1917*

HMS *Furious* made world history in 1917 when Dunning 'side-slipped' his Sopwith Pup onto the starboard side of the short forward flight deck, thus making the first landing of an aeroplane on a moving ship. *Furious* was steaming at 26 knots into a wind of 21 knots, providing Dunning with a headwind of 47 knots, and the landing was carried out with the assistance of the ship's crew, who grabbed the tail of his plane to help slow it down. Sadly Dunning was killed five days later while trying to repeat the landing in an even greater headwind, when his aircraft stalled and he was blown over the side of the ship. But his pioneering spirit proved that it was possible to land on a moving ship and the Royal Navy went on to perfect the concept of aircraft carriers. *Furious* was subsequently rebuilt with a longer aft flight deck to become the first genuine aircraft carrier equipped for landplanes. She became the longest-lived active carrier in the world and enjoyed great success in the Second World War despite being involved in a near head-on collision one night in the Atlantic with a troopship which passed so close it knocked off some the carrier's radio masts. HMS *Furious* was scrapped in 1949.

❏ ONLY airman to fall out of a plane and fall back in

Captain J H Hedley. Sunday 6 January 1918

After serving several months in the British infantry, Chicago-born Hedley transferred to the 20th Squadron of the Royal Flying Corps and was made a captain. On 6 January 1918 he was flying as navigator and observer in the open-cockpit, two-seater plane

Number 7255, piloted by Canadian Lieutenant Makepeace. At 15,000ft, while behind German lines, they encountered two enemy fighters – Makepeace immediately took evasive action by going into a steep vertical dive and the sudden 'G' force plucked Hedley out of his seat. As Makepeace levelled out about 300 feet below, he heard and felt loud thump from behind. Thinking he had been hit by German fire he looked back and saw Hedley clinging to the tail, struggling to climb back into his seat. The only explanation is that Hedley was carried along behind the plane by the slipstream and somehow sucked back onto the tail. In total Hedley survived 53 aerial combats before being shot down by the Red Baron, Manfred von Richthofen, and being taken prisoner. After the war he became a renowned speaker, famous for his 'thrillingly interesting' lecture, 'Rambling Through the Air'.

☆ FIRST member of the Royal Air Force
☆ FIRST air force to be independent of its nation's army or navy

H Edwards. Monday 1 April 1918

On 1 April 1918 the Royal Air Force was officially born with the merger of the Royal Flying Corps and the Royal Naval Air Service, becoming the first air force to be independent of its nation's army or navy. Existing personnel numbers were carried forward from the Royal Flying Corps. No 1 RFC was H Edwards, who enlisted in the army in 1895 and retired from the RFC on 16 October 1913, four and a half years before the formation of the RAF – so the first official member of the RAF never actually served in it. The first RAF member to serve was member No 5, W E Moore, who enlisted on 9 December 1889 and, by 1 April 1918, had become a warrant officer.

☆ FIRST woman to receive the Military Medal

Sara (aka Sadie) Bonnell. First World War. Sunday 19 May 1918

At the outbreak of the First World War Bonnell joined the First Aid Nursing Yeomanry (FANY) as an ambulance driver. On the night of 18/19 May 1918, when an ammunition dump close to St Omer was set on fire by enemy bombs, she and four other women spent five hours removing the wounded to safety, at constant risk from exploding ammunition and from the continuing bombardment. That night sixteen Military Medals and two Croixs de Guerre were awarded to FANY and voluntary aid detachments crews for their gallantry and conspicuous devotion to duty. General Sir Herbert Plumer, general officer commanding Second Army, presented the Military Medals in the field.

DID YOU KNOW?

Bonnell loved fast cars, and between the two world wars all her cars had a red fish mascot on the bonnet, a reminder of a senior British army officer's description of the FANY in France: 'Neither fish, flesh nor fowl but damned good red herring.'

❑ ONLY English soldier who had the chance but didn't kill Hitler

Pte Henry Tandey VC, Battle of Marcoing, France. First World War. Saturday 28 September 1918

Tandey was born in Leamington, Warwickshire, on 30 August 1891, the son of an ex-soldier. He joined the Green Howards in August 1910 at the age of eighteen and went on to serve in South Africa and Guernsey before the outbreak of the First World War.

He fought in the lst Battle of Ypres in October 1914, two years later he was wounded during the Battle of the Somme, and a year after that, in November 1917, he was wounded again at Passchendaele. On 26 July 1918 he was attached to the 5th Duke of Wellington Regiment, which galvanised him to become the highest-decorated private soldier of the war: he was awarded the Distinguished Conduct Medal on 28 August, the Military Medal on 12 September and the VC for conspicuous bravery at Marcoing on 28 September. With his regiment pinned down by machine-gun fire, 27-year-old Tandey crawled forward, located the forward machine-gun post and single-handedly destroyed it; then, still under fire from elsewhere, he managed to restore a plank bridge, enabling fellow troops to advance against the Germans; and finally, while surrounded and outnumbered, he led eight comrades in a successful bayonet charge which drove his attackers into the hands of the remainder of his company. During the battle a wounded German NCO limped straight towards Tandey out of the chaos. 'I took aim but couldn't shoot a wounded man,' he said later, 'so I let him go.' The man he let go was 29-year-old Lance Corporal Adolf Hitler, who was also highly decorated for an NCO, having won the Iron Cross First and Second Class. Hitler returned to Germany and eventual infamy, while Tandey returned to England a hero, and was decorated by George V at Buckingham Palace on 17 December 1919. Some newspaper reports of Tandey's VC were illustrated with a painting by the Italian artist Fortunino Matania of Tandey carrying a wounded soldier after the Battle of Ypres in 1914. Twenty years after the war, when British Prime Minister Neville Chamberlain met Hitler to sign the Munich Agreement, he was surprised to see that Hitler had a reproduction of the Matania painting. Hitler reputedly explained: 'That is the man who spared my life. That man came so near to killing me that I thought I should never see Germany again,' and asked

Chamberlain to pass on his thanks to Tandey. Chamberlain did as he was asked and so, on the eve of the Second World War, Tandey learned for the first time the identity of the man he had chosen to let live. After experiencing the Blitz on London and the destruction of Coventry first hand, Tandey told a journalist in 1940, 'If only I had known what he would turn out to be. When I saw all the people, women and children he had killed and wounded I was sorry to God I let him go.'

DID YOU KNOW?

Tandey was declared unfit to serve in the Second World War due to wounds sustained in the First. He died in Coventry on 20 December 1977 at the age of 86, and is interred at the British Cemetery in Marcoing alongside his fallen comrades. His VC is on display at the Green Howards regimental museum.

❑ ONLY British soldier to win five top gallantry medals without firing a shot

Lance Corporal William Coltman, North Staffordshire Regiment. First World War. Thursday 3 October 1918

On the night of 3/4 October 1918, on hearing that wounded men had been left behind during the retirement from Mannequin Hill, stretcher-bearer Coltman went forward alone three times in the face of fierce enfilade fire, found the casualties, dressed their wounds and carried some of them to safety on his back. He was the most highly-decorated NCO of the First World War – not only did he win the VC for his action at Mannequin Hill but also the Distinguished Conduct Medal and bar and the Military Medal and bar – a total of five separate gallantry awards won without firing a single shot.

❏ ONLY fighting soldier to spend the whole of the First World War in a cupboard

Trooper Patrick Fowler, 11th Hussars. First World War. Friday 18 October 1918

On 26 August 1914 Fowler was cut off from his regiment at the battle of Le Cateau, France. Wearing a stolen civilian coat he managed to dodge German patrols until he eventually met a woodcutter who guided him to a farmhouse owned by the woodcutter's mother-in-law, Madame Belmont-Gobert. Despite facing certain execution if caught harbouring a British soldier Mme Belmont-Gobert agreed to hide him. The only place available was a squat wardrobe, less than six feet high – it was to be Fowler's home for the next four years. The only time he was able to leave the wardrobe was for a few minutes late at night, giving him just enough time to stretch and eat. Two weeks after Fowler first hid in the wardrobe eight German soldiers were billeted in the house. Although they spent many hours drinking coffee and gossiping in the same room as the wardrobe, Fowler was never discovered. He did once dress up as a woman and tried hiding under a haystack, but after escaping death by inches when German soldiers plunged pitchforks into the hay, he returned to the comparative safety of the wardrobe. The next problem arose when the Germans requisitioned the whole house, forcing Mme Belmont-Gobert to move, with her belongings, to a small cottage nearby. Even then Fowler wasn't detected, despite the fact that a German soldier had to help move the wardrobe to the cottage with Fowler inside. Finally, on 18 October 1918, Allied troops reoccupied the village and Fowler was freed from his four-year, one-month and twenty-three-day ordeal. By coincidence, one of the first men he saw was one of his old officers from the 11th Hussars. Fowler was repatriated and Mme Belmont-Gobert was decorated for her bravery. Disbelievers of this amazing story are invited to view the actual wardrobe in which Fowler hid, which now stands in the Hussars' regimental museum in Winchester.

✳ LAST Allied soldier killed in the First World War

US Private Henry Gunther, Metz, France. First World War. Monday 11 November 1918

Hostilities officially ended the moment the Armistice was signed at 11:00 on 11 November 1918. As the moment approached Gunther, a private from Baltimore, Maryland, was with Company A, 313th Infantry, 79th Division of the US Army, advancing on Metz, near the German border, unaware that the war was about to end. Gunther's platoon ran into an ambush and, enraged by the machine-gun fire, Gunther charged the German position with fixed bayonet. At that moment a messenger arrived with word that the war was due to end at 11:00 but it was too late for Gunther, who was shot through the left temple and left side at 11:01. General Pershing's order of the day named him as the last American killed in the war. Some people argue that Gunther was killed after hostilities had officially ended, and was not therefore the last Allied soldier to be killed during the war – by that definition the dubious honour goes to Private G E Ellison of the 5th Royal Irish Lancers, who was shot dead about five seconds before 11:00.

DID YOU KNOW?

The first and last Allied soldiers killed in the First World War are buried within 100 yards of each other in the Military Cemetery at St Symphorian in Mons, France. The first to be killed was Private J Parr, of the Middlesex Regiment, on 23 August 1914.

✷ LAST time the British army used scaling ladders

Siege of Spin Baldak, Afghanistan. Third Afghan War. 03:00
Tuesday 27 May 1919

The fortress at Spin Baldak, four miles over the Afghan border
from Chaman, was surrounded by an outer wall 200 yards long
and fifteen feet high, within which was an even higher wall. The
British command ordered the 1st Gurkhas to take the south side
using scaling ladders. Twenty-two-year-old subaltern Ted Hughes
(later Brigadier) wrote a highly sarcastic, though probably
truthful account of what happened:

> 03.00 hours saw the mighty army move forward to the
> storming of the fortress. Everything was done in deathly
> silence – not a whisper was to rouse the unsuspecting
> Afghans. Indeed, the only sounds were the crashing of
> ammunition boxes and entrenching tools as the mules
> threw their loads and bolted into the night: every few
> seconds the air was split by the yells of some officer
> urging the men to greater silence or the despairing call of
> some NCO who had lost his section. A sound as of
> corrugated iron being dropped from a great height
> denoted that the scaling ladders were being loaded on
> the carts: with these two exceptions, no one would have
> had an inkling that several thousand armed men were
> pressing forward into the fray.

It turned out that the scaling ladders were too short but
fortunately the Afghan garrison commander decided against
confrontation and retreated with his army to the hills. One
wonders why it was deemed so important to capture the fort
since, after occupying it, strengthening the defences and
improving the water supply, the British handed it back to the
Afghans less than a month later.

☆ FIRST two-minute silence

United Kingdom, to commemorate the First World War. 11.00 Tuesday 11 November 1919

On 7 November 1919 King George V invited his people to join him four days later, at the eleventh hour of the eleventh day of the eleventh month, in commemorating the first anniversary of the Armistice by undertaking:

> ... for the brief space of two minutes a complete suspension of all our normal activities ... so that in perfect stillness, the thoughts of everyone may be concentrated on reverent remembrance of the glorious dead.

At 11:00 on 11 November the nation duly came to a silent standstill. The general public believed the two-minute silence was King George's own idea but it was actually based on an idea expressed by Australian journalist Edward George Honeyman in a letter published in the *London Evening News* on 8 May 1919. Honeyman, under the pen name Warren Foster, suggested that an appropriate commemoration would be:

> Five silent minutes of national remembrance. A very sacred intercession. Communion with the Glorious Dead who won us peace, and from the communion new strength, hope and faith in the morrow. Church services, too, if you will, but in the street, the home, the theatre, anywhere, indeed, where Englishmen and their women chance to be, surely in this five minutes of bitter-sweet silence there will be service enough.

The letter was read by Sir Percy Fitzpatrick who, on 27 October 1919, suggested the idea to George V. Honeyman's contribution was recognised when George V invited him to a rehearsal of the two minutes' silence at Buckingham Palace. A two-minute silence is now a universally-recognised symbol of remembrance.

✳ LAST British soldier to be executed by firing squad

Private James Daly, A Company, 1st Battalion of the Connaught Rangers, Dagashai, India. 06:00 Tuesday 2 November 1920

After the First World War Anglo-Irish relations declined and dissent began to spread within Irishmen serving in the British army. In Jullundur, north-west India, five men of the 1st Battalion Connaught Rangers mutinied, replacing the Union Jack with the flag of the Irish Republic and refusing to obey orders issued by the British army until British forces left Ireland. The mutiny was quickly quelled and the men were confined to live in stifling conditions under canvas in the oppressive heat. When news of the mutiny and the brutal treatment of the mutineers reached A Company, based at Solan, they too mutinied, and on 1 July 1920 Daly led some seventy soldiers in an attack on the camp's armoury. In the running battle that ensued two of the mutineers were shot. Daly cried out, 'If you want to know who the leader is, it is Private So and So Daly from Mullingar, Co Westmeath.' Again the mutiny was put down quickly, and ended with 61 mutineers being taken to Dagashai and put on trial; fourteen were sentenced to death. All but one had their sentences commuted to life imprisonment, but eyewitnesses testified that Daly had declared he was the leader, so his fate was sealed, and the 21-year-old was executed by firing squad in Dagashai Military Prison. In a last emotional letter he wrote to his mother:

> My Dearest Mother – I take this opportunity to let you know the dreadful news that I am to be shot on Tuesday morning the 2nd November … I am not afraid to die, it is only thinking of you. If you will be happy on earth, I will be happy in heaven. I am ready to meet my doom … I hope dear mother you will keep a stout heart, I know it is hard for you, but what can be done? I hope, mother,

you will get a mass said for the happy repose of your
fond son, Jim, taken from you for the sake of his country.
God Bless Ireland and all those at home.

Daly was eventually awarded the Victory and General Service
Medals for his active service for the British army during the First
World War.

☆ FIRST 'Unknown Soldier' buried

Westminster Abbey, London. 11:20 Thursday 11 November 1920

In 1916 the Reverend David Railton, a young English military
padre, returned to his billet at Earringham near Armentieres after
conducting a burial service. At the back of the billet he noticed a
grave marked with a white wooden cross inscribed: 'An Unknown
Soldier of the Black Watch', which inspired him to lead a campaign
to commemorate all the fallen of the First World War. On
7 November 1920 the corpses of four unidentified soldiers were
exhumed from the battlefields of Aisne, the Somme, Arras and
Ypres and taken to military headquarters at St Pol, where they were
laid a Nissen hut converted into a hastily-made chapel. At
midnight Brigadier General Wyatt, commander of the British
troops in France and Flanders, randomly selected one of the flag-
draped bodies. The other three were buried in a shell-hole on the
road to Albert while the chosen body was taken to Boulogne
accompanied by six barrels of earth from the battlefields, 'so that
he might lie in the earth so many gave their lives for'. The next day
the coffin was placed, along with a crusader's sword from George
V's private collection, in a second coffin made from an oak tree
which had stood at Hampton Court Palace, and wrapped in the
flag that Railton had used as an altar cloth during the war. (Known
as the Ypres or Padre's Flag, it now hangs in St George's Chapel,
Windsor Castle.) The coffin plate bore the inscription: 'A British

Warrior who fell in the Great War 1914-1918 for King and Country'. The coffin was taken to Dover aboard the destroyer HMS *Verdun* (named in honour of the battle, and whose ship's bell now hangs near the grave of the Unknown Soldier in Westminster Abbey), then by train to London's Victoria Station where it rested overnight. At 09:40 on Remembrance Day, 11 November, the body was placed on a gun carriage pulled by six black horses to begin its last journey to the Cenotaph ('empty tomb') and finally to rest at Westminster Abbey. Thirty-five thousand soldiers and policemen lined the 3,960 yard route containing vast crowds who stood in silent tears as the cortège passed. At 10:40 George V placed a wreath of red roses and bay leaves at the still-veiled Cenotaph with a signed handwritten note: 'In proud memory of those warriors who died unknown in the Great War. Unknown, and yet well known, as dying and behold they lived.' As Big Ben struck the last note of 11:00 the king pressed the button that unveiled the new memorial by releasing the Union Flags that covered it. The king then followed the cortège on foot to Westminster Abbey, where nearly 1,000 widows and mothers of the fallen waited in silence. The coffin was borne aloft by members of the Coldstream Guards and slow-marched through a guard of honour made up of 100 holders of the Victoria Cross. As the coffin was lowered into its final resting place the king sprinkled some the earth taken from the battlefields, and the remaining soil was then poured over it. Finally the grave was covered with the Union Flag and the Actors' Pall, given by actors to remember their fellow artists who had died in the war. At the end of the week the Actors' Pall was replaced by a temporary slab of Tournai Marble inscribed: 'A British Warrior who fell in the Great War 1914-1918 For King and Country Greater Love Hath No Man Than This.' A year later a slab of black Belgian granite replaced the Tournai Marble. Its long inscription concludes: 'They Buried Him Among The Kings Because He Had Done Good Toward God and Toward His House.'

DID YOU KNOW?

Other nations followed Britain's example in commemorating unknown soldiers, but the tradition could now be at an end in the USA. In 1998 the Pentagon announced that the Unknown Warriors from both Korea and Vietnam had been identified by DNA testing. The last American Unknown Soldier buried at Arlington National Cemetery was named as Lieutenant Michael Blassie, a 24-year-old air force fighter pilot who was shot down near An Loc on 11 May 1972. Blassie's remains were exhumed, returned to his family in Saint Louis, Missouri, and finally re-interred at Jefferson Barracks National Cemetery. The marker at Arlington was replaced with one that read: 'Honoring and Keeping Faith with America's Missing Servicemen.'

✻ LAST Royal Navy left-handed salute

Royal Navy. Saturday 20 January 1923

The army abolished the left-handed salute in July 1918, and five years later the navy abolished the left-handed personal salute of a naval rating when meeting an officer. The amended regulation, with instructions on how to salute, was published in *The Times*, though one wonders how many ratings read that newspaper:

> The naval salute is to be made by bringing up the right hand to the cap hat, naturally and smartly but not hurriedly, with the thumb and fingers straight and close together, elbow in line with the shoulder, hand and forearm in line, the thumb being in line with the outer edge of the right eyebrow, with the palm of the hand turned to the left.

Six days later an objection appeared in *The Times* letters column from Colonel C J L Davidson, The Manor House, Eglinton,

Co Londonderry, complaining of the change. He pointed out that when the saluted pass right hand to right hand their elbows would collide:

> What is the object in abolishing the left-handed salute in the Navy and Army? Common sense and smartness have hitherto upheld the salute being made with the hand farthest from the person being saluted. Under the new order nothing looks or is more clumsy than the salute with the right hand when the saluted pass right hand to right hand. Elbows must collide, and eyes and faces cannot conveniently be timed in the saluting direction.

✳ LAST lance in the British army

Army Order 392. Thursday 13 January 1927

The success of Napoleon's lancer regiments during the Battle of Waterloo led directly to the formation of the first British lancer regiment in 1816, at which time lances were sixteen feet long and made of ash impregnated with a mixture of linseed oil and tar. In 1829 the British army lance was reduced to nine feet one inch, and in 1868 ash was replaced by bamboo, which was tougher and lighter. Then, in 1927, Army Order 392 stated that the lance was abolished as a weapon and was only to be used for ceremonial purposes.

✳ LAST survivor of the Charge of the Light Brigade

Edwin Hughes, Blackpool, England. Wednesday 18 May 1927

In 1852 Hughes, a 21-year-old shoemaker, joined the 13th Light Dragoons as a private, and on 25 October 1854, having attained the rank of troop sergeant-major, he rode in the Charge of the Light Brigade at the Battle of Balaclava (*see 1854*). Hughes's horse was shot from under him and he was 'damaged about the face and left leg but not seriously'. He later said, 'We just did our duty without any thought of glory, and, of course, as in all wars many of our lot paid the supreme price.' He continued to serve in the Crimean campaign until being discharged in 1873, after which he became known as 'Balaclava Ned'. He died on 18 May 1927 at the age of 96, having outlived the penultimate survivor of the Charge of the Light Brigade by four years. On 25 October 1992, the 138th anniversary of the Charge, a plaque was placed on the house where he was born in Mount Street, Wrexham.

☆ FIRST Anderson Shelters

Tober Street and Carlsbad Street Islington, London, England.
Saturday 25 February 1939

The development of the Anderson Shelter is usually attributed to the then home secretary (Sir) John Anderson. On 10 November 1938 Anderson presented his idea for a cheap domestic bomb shelter to engineer William Paterson who, along with his co-director Oscar Carl Kerrison, produced the first blueprint within a week and the first model within a fortnight. Anderson reportedly tested the prototype by jumping on it with both feet! Comprising fourteen sheets of corrugated iron, each shelter formed a curved shell six feet high, four and half feet wide and six and half feet long. It was buried to a depth of four feet and then covered with at least fifteen inches of soil. On 25 February 1939 the first Anderson shelters were delivered by Islington Borough Council to the residents of Tober Street and Carlsbad Street. With typical cockney humour the recipient of the first shelter, Mrs Treadwell, said, 'I hope we shall never have to use it … Still, if trouble does come, it will be better than nothing.' She then added, 'We can always use it as a summer house.' In the event Anderson shelters saved thousands of lives during the Blitz. Many shelters became garden features, usually sited at the bottom of the garden as far as possible from the house in case the house collapsed. They were issued free to anyone earning less than £250 a year, and at a charge of £7 for those with higher incomes. In total 2,250,000 were erected. At the end of 1941, an American journalist wrote that 'there was a greater danger of being hit by a vegetable marrow falling off the roof of an air-raid shelter than of being struck by a bomb'. Oddly, by 1962 the shelters that had once provided a safe haven were regarded as a menace, particularly derelict communal shelters in parks, which were the scene of 'murder, rape, violence [and] babies found dead'.

❑ ONLY dog to be officially enlisted in the Royal Navy
❑ ONLY member of the Royal Navy excused by Admiralty orders from wearing a cap at any time

Able Seaman Just Nuisance, RN. Friday 25 August 1939

'Just Nuisance' was a huge pedigree Great Dane born in Rondebosch, a suburb of Cape Town, South Africa, on Thursday, 1 April 1937 – but his story is no April Fool joke. The young pup was sold to Benjamin Chaney, who moved to Simon's Town to run the United Services Institute (USI) which was frequented by Royal Navy personnel from the Simon's Town Naval Base. The sailors soon adopted the Great Dane, spoiling him with pies and beer, and he seemed to recognise his mates by their uniforms – he usually ignored or growled at other servicemen, including naval officers, who dressed differently from the ratings. Although well loved, he earned his name Nuisance because of his habit of lying around sunning himself and getting in the way of sailors going about their duties. Nuisance would regularly follow the naval liberty men when they went by train to Cape Town, some 22 miles north by rail, and he became renowned for finding drunken sailors on the train and escorting them back to their bunks in Simon's Town. Sailors would try to hide Nuisance from the ticket collector but he was often discovered and bumped off at the next station, where he would wait and board the next train to continue his journey. Angry railway officials warned Chaney that they would have Nuisance put down if he persisted in boarding trains. This created a massive outcry, and in August 1939 the ratings decided to enlist Nuisance in the Royal Navy, which would entitle him to a free rail pass. When the clerk asked for the dog's Christian name he was told he didn't have one, he was 'just Nuisance' – thus his official Christian name became Just. His trade was entered as 'Bone Crusher' and his religious denomination as 'Scrounger' (later amended to Canine Divinity League [Anti-Vivisection]). He signed his enlistment form with a paw mark, and after a medical examination he was duly declared fit for active duty. He was quickly promoted from 'Ordinary Seaman' to 'Able Seaman', conveniently entitling him to naval rations! Just Nuisance assisted the war effort by 'marrying' another Great Dane, Adinda – two of their five puppies were auctioned for war funds by the mayor of Cape Town. However, he also lived up to his name, as revealed by his conduct sheet:

> Travelling on the railways without a pass. Punishment Awarded: Confined to the banks of Froggy Pond, Lily Pool, with all lamp posts removed.
> Did sleep in an improper place, namely in a bed in the Petty Officers' dormitory. Punishment Awarded: Deprived of bones for seven days.

His most serious offence was fighting and killing the mascots on HMS *Shropshire* and HMS *Redoubt*, though he was exonerated on both occasions when it was proved that he was defending himself after the other dogs attacked first. On Saturday 1 January 1944 he was discharged from the navy at HMS *Afrikander*, where he had been stationed since 1940. He then developed the dangerous habit of jumping off moving buses and lorries, seriously injuring his back legs and damaging his sciatic nerve, as a result of which a vet recommended he be put down. On 1 April 1944, his seventh birthday, Just Nuisance was taken by lorry to Simon's Town Naval Hospital for the fatal injection, and at 11:30 the following day he was laid to rest with full military honours at Klaver Camp. For years a simple granite gravestone marked his grave but there is now a beautiful statue of him overlooking and guarding the harbour. The inscription at its base reads: 'Just Nuisance A.B. Loyal friend and companion of the sailors who called at this port during the Second World War. Remembered with affection.' At his feet lies the cap which, uniquely, he never had to wear.

❑ ONLY world war started by a hoax

Gleiwitz Radio Station, then in Germany on the Polish border (now part of Poland). 23:00 Thursday 31 August 1939

Gestapo Chief Reinhard Heydrich appointed SS Officer Alfred Naujocks to lead this audacious hoax, code-named Operation Himmler. Twelve German civilian prisoners were injected with tranquillisers, removed from jail and dressed in Polish Army uniforms. Then Naujocks led them and a few SS men, also dressed in Polish uniforms, to a German radio station in Gleiwitz. Once there all the prisoners were shot one by one and left positioned as if attacking the radio station. Then, at 23:00, ensuring that the radio transmitters were broadcasting the action, Naujocks fired shots into the ceiling and an SS man who spoke fluent Polish screamed defiant slogans into the microphone. The following day German newspapers published photographs of 'Polish soldiers' killed while supposedly attacking the station. The newspaper reports of the faked attack outraged the duped German public and were used as the pretext to invade Poland, heralding the start of the Second World War.

☆ FIRST moment of the Second World War

German-Polish border. 04:36 Friday 1 September 1939

Using the radio station hoax (*see previous entry*) to justify the invasion of Poland, Hitler began the Second World War at 04:36, with the Luftwaffe's Stuka dive-bombers attacking Polish communications centres and airfields in thick fog. The Poles had scattered their planes among small makeshift airfields which, combined with the fog, made locating them tricky for the Germans. Nine minutes later, at 04:45, German land forces crashed through the Polish frontier. About a million troops, comprising forty-one infantry divisions and fourteen Panzer and motorised divisions, began their lighting advance across Poland. Polish resistance was courageous but doomed. In sixteen days the Germans had reached Warsaw which, after a heroic stand, capitulated on 27 September. The Germans never formally declared war on Poland.

☆ FIRST British fatality of the Second World War

PC George Southworth, Harley Street, London. Second World War. Sunday 3 September 1939

On 3 September 1939 Britain declared war on Germany, and that evening an air raid warning was heard throughout London's West End. Police Constable Southworth, on patrol in Harley Street, noticed a light shining from a third-floor window. Knowing that any light can be a target to enemy bombers, he was determined to extinguish it so he knocked at the door but got no answer. Showing exemplary devotion to duty he then climbed a drain pipe to reach the lit room but fell from the third floor and was killed. Ironically, the air raid warning proved to be a false alarm.

☆ **FIRST** Allied shot of the Second World War in the Far East

Point Nepean, Port Phillip Bay, Melbourne, Australia. Second World War. 21:15 Sunday 3 September 1939

The first Allied shot of the war in the Far East was fired by Australians on Australians. The coaster *Woniora*, returning from Tasmania under the command of Captain F N Smale, entered Port Philip Bay, Melbourne, at 21:15 on 3 September 1939 and was ordered to heave-to for inspection. Smale identified his ship but failed to stop – until a 100-pound shell fired from the twin 6-inch gun emplacement at Point Nepean whistled across his bows. Coincidentally, the same gun emplacement fired the first Australian shot of the First World War on 5 August 1914 when, just hours after war was declared, it fired on the German steamer *Pfalz*, which was attempting to leave Australian waters. The captured vessel then became the Australian troopship HMT *Boorara*.

☆ **FIRST** time Spitfires fired their guns in anger
☆ **FIRST** friendly fire fatality of the Second World War
☆ **FIRST** RAF fatality of the Second World War

Battle of Barking Creek, London. Second World War. Wednesday 6 September 1939

Poor communication on the ground, coupled with the fact that British fighter planes were not fitted with IFF equipment (Identification Friend or Foe) meant that the first planes to be shot down by the legendary Spitfire were a pair of British Hurricanes. An air raid siren – which subsequently proved to be a false alarm – led to the scrambling of several Hurricanes of 56 Squadron from North Weald airfield, followed shortly afterwards by two reserve Hurricanes piloted by Frank Rose and Montague Hulton-Harrop. Meanwhile Spitfires of 74 Squadron were scrambled from Hornchurch airfield with the erroneous information that the two reserve Hurricanes were enemy aircraft. Spitfire pilots Paddy Byrne and John Freeborn shot down the Hurricanes, Freeborn's shots killing Hulton-Harrop, who thus became the first RAF fatality and the first friendly fire fatality of the war. Byrne and Freeborn were both exonerated by the court martial that followed, and the production of IFF equipment was made a top priority. The origin of the name of this 'battle' is uncertain, given that it took place nowhere near Barking Creek.

☆ FIRST British aircraft to shoot down an enemy aircraft in the Second World War

Fairey Battle bomber K9243, Aachen, Germany. Wednesday 20 September 1939

Many sources cite the shooting down of a German Dornier 18 by British Skuas on 26 September as the first British aerial victory of the war but that should technically be listed as the first to be confirmed. Six days earlier, three RAF Fairey Battle bombers of 88 Squadron took off at 10:00 from Mourmelon-Le-Grand, France, for a reconnaissance flight over Aachen, Germany, where they were engaged by three Messerschmitt Bf109 fighters. The Messerschmitts shot down two of the British planes but the third, piloted by Flying Officer L H Baker and crewed by Sergeant L H Letchford and Aircraftman Class 1 C A Edwards, returned fire, gunner Letchford claiming a Bf109 shot down. This was not immediately confirmed – hence the confusion over the 26 September 'kill' – but French sources later supplied evidence to support Letchford's claim, which was eventually confirmed as the first British aerial victory of the war.

☆ **FIRST** British capital ship to be lost in the Second World War

HMS Royal Oak, *Scapa Flow, Orkney. Second World War. 00:16 Saturday 14 October 1939*

The battleship *Royal Oak* was sunk at her moorings at the British Home Fleet Naval Base in Scapa Flow, Orkney Islands, by three torpedoes fired at 00:16 from the German submarine U-47. The *Royal Oak* rolled over and sank in less than fifteen minutes, with the loss of 833 of her crew of 1,234. The wreck is a designated war grave, which means that all diving or other unauthorised forms of exploration are prohibited under the Protection of Military Remains Act 1986, but divers do visit the sunken ship – every year on 14 October Royal Navy divers place a White Ensign on the hull.

☆ **FIRST** RAF air raid of the Second World War
✻ **LAST** RAF bombing raid without a fighter escort

Wilhelmshaven, Germany. Second World War. 09:30 Monday 18 December 1939

The first RAF raid of the war was a bloody disaster. At 09:30 twenty-four Wellington bombers of No 3 Group, RAF Bomber Command, took off from various airfields in East Anglia each armed with three 500-pound bombs. The myth that the bombers were invincibile was still believed, so they were unescorted as they headed for their target, the German naval port of Wilhelmshaven. An hour later two planes returned to base with engine trouble. The remainder of the group was spotted thirty miles off the German coast by the Freya radar station but the reading was dismissed as a flock of seagulls because no one believed that the RAF would launch an attack in such crystal-clear daylight conditions. Visual contact was established as the bombers crossed the coast but they were flying so high that anti-aircraft fire was ineffectual, while six Messerschmitts sent to intercept them were told to abandon the chase for fear of being shot down by their own ground crews. Thus the bombers reached their target unscathed, but when they arrived they were unable to carry out their mission: the pilots were under strict orders not to cause civilian casualties, but German homes were so close to docks that any bombing would inevitably kill innocent civilians. They turned round to return to base, dropping a few bombs on German ships as they went, but now the Messerschmitts returned, their pilots well aware that Wellingtons were vulnerable to attack from the side – an angle not protected by the bombers' guns. It became a turkey shoot – at a cost of just two fighters the Germans shot down twelve Wellingtons, killing 53 British airmen. Only ten planes made it home, the last one arriving at 16:00 after six and a half hours of terror. Never again would British bombers make a raid without escort. By the end of the war Bomber Command lost 9,000 aircraft, with 55,000 aircrew killed.

☆ FIRST British civilian fatalities from direct military action in the Second World War

Frederick and Dorothy Gill, Upper Victoria Road, Clacton-on-Sea, Essex. Second World War. Tuesday 30 April 1940

On 29 April 1940 a German Heinkel 111 bomber on a mine-laying sortie off the east coast of England became lost in heavy fog. Just before midnight it crossed the coast near Bawdsey in Suffolk, and coastal anti-aircraft batteries at Bawdsey, Felixstowe and Harwich opened fire. Shells exploding beneath the Heinkel damaged the controls and the pilot desperately circled Clacton-on-Sea and Holland-on-Sea looking for a landing site before flying out to sea again and then returning at a much lower altitude. Finally it hit the chimneys of a number of houses before crashing into the Gill family home in Upper Victoria Road, Clacton-on-Sea. The live mine it was carrying exploded, destroying the house and killing Frederick and Dorothy Gill, who became the first of more than 60,000 civilians killed in England during the war. They were buried in an unmarked grave in the Burrs Road Cemetery. The grave was discovered in 1994 and five years later, on the 59th anniversary of their deaths, a Commonwealth War Graves Commission headstone was erected and dedicated.

✳ LAST BEF evacuee to leave Dunkirk

General Sir Harold Alexander (later 1st Earl Alexander of Tunis)
Dunkirk, France. Second World War. 23:40 Sunday 2 June 1940

Alexander's promotion to major-general in 1937, at the age of 45, made him the youngest general in the British army, but it was the evacuation of the British Expeditonary Force from Dunkirk which brought his name to prominent public notice. During the three days under his command 110,000 Allied troops were evacuated, and before heading home Alexander repeatedly risked his life to ensure no BEF troops were left behind, zigzagging round the harbour in a motorboat, under constant fire, to check the beach. At 23:40 Alexander left Dunkirk thinking he was the last BEF evacuee, and the few remaining naval officers began loading newly-arrived French troops. At about 02:00 three British soldiers who had somehow been left leapt aboard the trawler *Yorkshire Lass* – the last recorded BEF evacuees. British ships returned the following night to evacuate French troops, the last warship to leave being HMS *Shikari* at 03:40 on 4 June. The last vessel of all to leave was motor torpedo boat 107 commanded by Lieutenant John Cameron, who later wrote: 'The whole scene was filled with a sense of finality and death; the curtain was ringing down on a great tragedy.'

* LAST successful invasion of the British Isles

Sark, Channel Islands. Second World War. Thursday 4 July 1940

On 15 June, after the fall of France, the British government concluded that it would be impossible to defend the Channel Islands and decided instead to demilitarise them and not resist a German invasion on the basis that occupying the islands would require considerable German resources for no strategic advantage. By 21 June all troops, most of the children, most of the men of military age and even some livestock had been evacuated. However, the Germans clearly expected some resistance, and sent in the Luftwaffe on 28 June as a show of force, killing 44 civilians in bombing raids on St Peter Port, Guernsey, and St Helier, Jersey. On 30 June the Luftwaffe dropped leaflets demanding the surrender of the islands, and later that night the Bailiff of Guernsey handed control of the island to a group of German officers who landed at Guernsey airport. On 1 July the Germans occupied Jersey in a similarly polite take over, Alderney (which had been completely evacuated) was occupied on 2 July and Sark on 4 July. The occupation lasted five years, ending on 9 May 1945 when the Germans surrendered without a fight to two Royal Navy destroyers sent to liberate the islands.

❑ ONLY person to volunteer to be imprisoned at Auschwitz

Witold Pilecki. Second World War. Saturday 21 September 1940

As a member of the 41st Polish Infantry Division, Pilecki was instrumental in destroying seven German tanks and shooting down two aircraft at the start of the Second World War before founding the resistance movement known as *Tajna Armia*

Polska ('Secret Polish Army') on 9 November 1939. In 1940 he became the only person known to have volunteered to be imprisoned at Auschwitz, which he did in order to organise inmate resistance and gather intelligence on what was then thought to be an internment camp. His colleagues in *Tajna Armia Polska* gave him the false identity of Tomasz Serafinski, and on 19 September 1940 he deliberately allowed himself to be rounded up by the Germans, after which he was tortured, sent to Auschwitz and tattooed with the number 4859. The following year he organised the *Zwiazek Organizacji Wojskowych* (Union of Military Organisations) within the camp to improve morale, disseminate information and even organise supply lines from the outside world, distributing medical, food and clothing supplies. Pilecki also sent regular reports of the atrocities being perpetrated inside the camp, which were forwarded to British intelligence. He hoped that these reports would prompt the Allies or the Polish Home Army to liberate the camp but on the night of 26-27 April 1943, having realised this wasn't going to happen, he escaped with two fellow inmates, hoping that his personal testimony would convince the Allies to mount a rescue operation. However, his reports were deemed to be exaggerated and Allied air cover for a Home Army attack too risky so no liberation attempt was made. Pilecki then joined an underground anti-communist organization within the Home Army called *NIE* ('NO'), which had been formed to prepare for resistance to Soviet occupation. After the war he began documenting atrocities committed under the communist regime and on 8 May 1947 he was arrested, tortured, and convicted on false evidence of spying. On 25 May 1948 he was executed at Mokotow Prison in Warsaw. He was rehabilitated in 1990 after the fall of the communist regime, and in 1995 he was posthumously awarded the Order of *Polonia Restituta*.

* **LAST** exchange of fire with enemy combatants on mainland British soil

Battle of Graveney Marshes, Kent, England. Second World War. Friday 27 September 1940.

During the Battle of Britain the RAF shot down a Junkers 88 piloted by Fritz Ruhlandt, who managed to land his stricken plane on Graveney Marshes. The London Irish Rifles, billetted in the nearby Sportsman Inn, arrived on the scene expecting the crew to surrender but instead the Germans opened up with two machine guns. The London Irish returned fire and eventually the Germans gave themselves up, announcing that there was a bomb on the plane set to explode shortly. Captain Cantopher of the London Irish defused the bomb (winning a Military Medal for capturing the crew and saving the plane, vital for intelligence) and the 'Battle of Graveney Marsh' concluded with no fatalities. Some people cite this as 'the last battle on mainland British soil' but, whilst it was the last exchange of fire with enemy combatants on mainland British soil (and the only German-British fighting encounter of the Second World War on mainland British soil) it was not a true battle, so that honour remains with the Battle of Culloden. (*See 1746*)

❑ **ONLY** Luftwaffe prisoner of war to escape and make it back to Germany

Franz von Werra, Ogdensburg, New York State, USA. Second World War. c19:00 Friday 24 January 1941

Fighter pilot von Werra is often referred to as the only Axis prisoner of war to succeed in escaping and returning to the Reich – in fact several others also succeeded in doing so, but it is true that von Werra was the only German airman to perform the feat. By

September 1940 he had claimed nine combat victories (though five were never confirmed) but on 5 September, during the Battle of Britain, his Bf 109 was shot down over Kent by Pilot Officer Gerald Stapleton of No 603 Squadron. Von Werra crash-landed in a field, was captured by the unarmed cook from a nearby army unit, and eventually dispatched to POW Camp No1, at Grizedale Hall in Cumbria. He made his first escape on 7 October during a daytime exercise walk outside the camp – while a passing fruit cart provided a diversion and other German prisoners covered for him, von Werra slipped over a dry-stone wall into a field. At 23:00 on 10 October two Home Guard soldiers found him sheltering in a small stone hut but he quickly disappeared into the night. Two days later he was spotted climbing a 1,200-foot hill overlooking the Duddon Valley and police recaptured him despite his near-successful attempt to camouflage himself by covering himself in freezing mud. After 21 days of solitary confinement he was transferred to Camp No 10 in Swanwick, Derbyshire, where he joined a team digging an escape tunnel, and at 21:00 on 20 December, armed with forged identity papers and under the cover of anti-aircraft fire and the singing of the camp choir, he escaped again, this time with four others. The others were quickly recaptured but von Werra, wearing a borrowed flying suit, posed as Captain Van Lott, a Dutch RAF pilot who had recently been shot down. With admirable bravado he convinced staff at a local railway station to arrange transport to RAF Hucknall where, while his story was being verified, he dashed to the nearest hangar and told a mechanic that he was cleared for a test flight in a Hurricane. He was arrested as he was inside the cockpit, about to start the engines. In January 1941 von Werra was shipped to Halifax, Nova Scotia, with 1,050 other German POWs, and during the voyage he spent long periods in a bath of freezing sea water, hardening himself in case he spotted an opportunity to leap overboard on arrival. In Canada the POWs were put on a prison train destined for the north shore of

Lake Superior, Ontario. At a station stop just before dawn on 24 January, while guards were distracted by fellow prisoners, von Werra audaciously dived head-first from the window of the train into deep snow, and his absence wasn't noticed until the next afternoon. Von Werra had left the train at Smiths Falls, just 30 miles from the St Lawrence River which formed the border with the USA (which at that time was still neutral). He hitched a ride then made his way to the river, where he could see the distant lights of Ogdensburg and freedom. At 19:00 he took a chance. He started to walk across the frozen river but, only a quarter of a mile from safety, he encountered broken ice, which left him no choice but to return to the Canadian bank. There he found a rowing boat which he prised out of the snow and dragged back to the open channel. Luckily for the oarless von Werra, the current carried him to the American shore, where he turned himself in. The Ogdensburg police charged him with vagrancy, and the immigration authorities with entering the country illegally, so von Werra contacted the local German consul and began spinning stories that startled the American public. The Canadians tried to have him extradited to face the charge of stealing a $35 rowing boat. When it became clear US authorities were negotiating his extradition to Canada the German vice-consul helped spirit him, disguised as a Mexican labourer, across the border into Mexico. Von Werra proceeded to Rio de Janeiro, Barcelona, Rome and finally arrived back in Germany on 18 April 1941, where Hitler awarded him the Iron Cross, and he became a national hero, later writing a survival booklet that became standard issue to all German aircrews. Returning to the Luftwaffe, von Werra was deployed on the Russian front, where he was credited with eight more victories, and later flew fighter patrols over the North Sea. On 25 October 1941 von Werra disappeared during a routine patrol north of Vlissingen in the Netherlands, in an accident due to 'engine failure and the pilot's carelessness'. It was officially announced he had been killed in action.

☆ FIRST British parachute raid

Operation Colossus, Tragino Aqueduct, Italy. Second World War. Monday 10 February 1941

On 22 June 1940 Winston Churchill issued a memo stating that Britain should have a corps of at least 5,000 parachute troops. Two days later Major John Rock of the Royal Engineers was posted to the RAF parachute training school to 'take charge of the military organisation of British Airborne Forces'. He was given no further information as to policy or mission; he had no men, no aircraft, and had never seen a parachute in his life. Within eight months the first British parachute raid took place, carried out by 35 men, all volunteers, who made up 'X' Troop, No 2 Commando II Special Air Service Battalion. (Not to be confused with the SAS [*see 1941*]: this battalion was formed from No 2 Commando and subsequently became the foundation of the Parachute Regiment as 1st Battalion, The Parachute Regiment.) The objective of Operation Colossus was to sabotage Italy's Tragino Aqueduct. During the night of 10 February, five Whitleys arrived over the target and dropped their paratroops from 400 feet – a sixth plane failed to find the target and dropped its paratroops into the next valley, where they were unable to be of any use in the raid. This meant a shortfall of explosives – a problem exacerbated by the discovery that the aqueduct was made of concrete, not brick as expected. Undeterred, 'X' Troop pressed on with its mission and, at 00.30, half the Tragino Aqueduct collapsed under 800 pounds of explosive. An hour later the troop split into three parties to attempt a coastal rendezvous with the submarine HMS *Triumph*, a hazardous journey across difficult terrain and through hostile villages and towns. All three parties were discovered and all but one of the raiding party imprisoned – their Italian interpreter, formerly a waiter at London's Savoy Hotel, was shot as a traitor.

☆ **FIRST** German submarine captured by the British in the Second World War

U-110, Battle of the Atlantic. Second World War. Thursday 8 May 1941

U-110 had already sunk two ships of the OB318 Atlantic convoy when its periscope was spotted. British corvette HMS *Aubrietia* immediately dropped depth charges, and destroyers HMS *Bulldog* and HMS *Broadway* headed for the location. When the destroyers arrived there was short but fierce exchange of fire before the surviving German crew surrendered to *Bulldog*'s captain, Joe Baker-Cresswell, who realised there was a chance of gleaning information from the U-boat and keeping his possession of that information secret from the Germans. He put the prisoners below decks on the *Bulldog*, where they could not see what was happening, and ordered a thorough search of U-110. The boarding party removed equipment, charts, log books and instruments as well as – crucially, on Baker-Cresswell's astute orders – noting the tuning positions of all U-110's radio sets. *Bulldog* then began to tow the stricken U-boat back to port but the weather worsened and the next morning U-110 sank. However, the disappointment was short lived – when intelligence officers examined the prize they were astounded. Not only had *Bulldog* retrieved U-110's Enigma cipher machine with the settings for 9 May still intact but also the current code book for all U-boats' short signal sighting reports. This meant that, without the Germans realising, British naval command knew the whereabouts of the German fleet. The intelligence yielded had a huge impact not only on the Battle of the Atlantic but also on the land campaign in Africa, changing the course of the war. Not surprisingly this outstanding success was kept secret, and it wasn't until 1959 that the world found out about what was arguably the single most important event of the Second World War.

☆ FIRST RAF prisoner of war to make the 'home run' from Germany

Captain (later Air Marshal Sir) Harry Burton, Stalag Luft 1, Barth, Baltic. Second World War. Tuesday 27 May 1941

In September 1940, after a successful operation to drop incendiaries on Black Forest targets, Burton's Wellington bomber was hit by anti-aircraft fire. Ordering his crew to bale out, he remained on board destroying secret equipment before baling out himself and landing in a Belgian swamp. After burying his parachute he covered his uniform in mud and pretended to be a Belgian worker, despite which he was soon captured and incarcerated in Stalag Luft I. The camp contained a highly active escape committee which, during the winter and spring, attempted over fifty escapes. Burton was involved in digging a tunnel for one of these escapes but the tunnel was discovered and he was punished with ten days' solitary confinement. While in solitary he managed to loosen the cell bars, and in the early hours of 27 May 1941 he succeeded in climbing out of his cell. He then burrowed under one gate, clambered over a second and, avoiding the dog patrols whose timings he had memorised, made his escape over a ten-foot wire fence. At daylight he rested in woods and that night he clung to the belly of a railway box car with his back on an axle, riding all the way to the coast where he knew a ferry to Sweden was due to depart the following afternoon. When he arrived in Sweden he was promptly arrested and imprisoned until the Air Ministry confirmed his identity and arranged for him to be flown home. After Burton retired in 1973 he was chairman of the board of Princess Marina House, an RAF Benevolent Fund home. One day an ex-navigator arrived there and asked for Burton, who instantly recognised Duncan McFarlane, who had been with him when they were shot down – they hadn't seen each other for 47 years.

☆ FIRST operation by the SAS
❏ ONLY SAS operation of the Second World War to be deployed by parachute

Western Desert, North Africa. Second World War. Monday 17 November 1941

In the early days the SAS (Special Air Service), founded by David Stirling, was known as L Detachment of the non-existent Special Air Service Brigade. Its prime function was to parachute behind German lines and destroy aircraft on the ground, but only one of the new unit's operations during the Second World War in North Africa involved parachutes. Operation Squatter took place on the moonless night of 16/17 November 1941, and was a single option mission to secure air superiority for the British 8th Army 24 hours before the commencement of the army main offensive Operation Crusader. This first venture for the fledgling SAS involved simultaneous airborne attacks by five Bristol Bombay aircraft of 216 Squadron, on five separate airfields, involving seven officers and 57 other ranks. The operation was a disaster. Because of a sandstorm with winds blowing at over ninety miles per hour, the parachutists were blown all over the desert. Only one detachment actually reached its target, and all of those men were killed – only four officers and eighteen other ranks emerged from the desert alive. Stirling changed tactics, and cancelled any more airborne operations in favour of long land attacks on airfields. The success of this change in tactics was astonishing, and the SAS went on to destroy more enemy aircraft in the Western Desert than the RAF.

DID YOU KNOW?

The name 'Special Air Service' was first used the previous year by the fledgling Parachute Regiment. (*see 10 February1941*)

☆ **FIRST** prisoner of war captured by Americans in the Second World War

Kazuo Sakamaki, Pearl Harbor. Second World War. Sunday 7 December 1941

As an ensign in the Japanese imperial navy, Kazuo Sakamaki and crewman Kyoshi Inagaki were aboard a tiny 'midget' submarine that was pummelled by American depth charges and cannon shells at the entrance to Pearl Harbor on the morning of 7 December 1941. Sakamaki and Inagaki were overcome by battery fumes and spent the remainder of that fateful day unconscious and drifting. When they came to, they found themselves near Waimanalo Beach. To avoid their submarine being captured they set a timed explosive charge and tried to swim ashore. Inagaki died in the attempt, and Sakamaki was captured by Hawaiian soldier David Akui. All the rest of the midget submariners perished in the attack, and Sakamaki was deeply humiliated to be taken alive as Prisoner of War No 1. In disgrace, he burned himself with cigarettes in prison on Sand Island and demanded to be allowed to commit suicide. American guards declined. His submarine was also captured intact and became a valuable war-bond recruiting tool, touring the United States. Sakamaki spent the rest of the war as an American POW, and when the war ended, he was repatriated to Japan deeply committed to pacifism. The Japanese considered his survival to be a disgrace, so he wrote an explanatory account of his experiences, entitled *I Attacked Pearl Harbor,* but from then on refused to discuss the war. He worked as a senior executive with the Toyota Motor Corporation and retired in 1987. In 1991, Sakamaki travelled to Texas to attend a historical conference where he was reunited with his submarine for the first time in fifty years; he wept. He died, aged 81, on 29 November 1999.

☆ FIRST US forces arrive in Australia

Brisbane, Australia. Second World War. Wednesday 24 December 1941

The first of almost one million US servicemen to pass through Australia during the Second World War arrived at Brisbane on Christmas Eve 1941. The war severely depleted the female Australian population – some 7,000 Australian women married American boyfriends and travelled to the USA as war brides.

☆ FIRST air raid on Australia

Darwin, Australia. Second World War. 09:58 Thursday 19 February 1942

Collectively, the Japanese air raids on Darwin from 1942–3 were the largest aerial attacks mounted by a foreign power against Australia. In the first attack the Japanese launched two waves of planes, the first wave of 188 fighters and bombers taking off at 08:45 from four aircraft carriers used in the attack on Pearl Harbor: *Akagi*, *Kaga*, *Hiryu* and *Soryu*. At about 09:15 the planes were spotted by a missionary on Bathurst and Melville Islands, and Darwin was warned at least twice by radio – but unfortunately ten US Kittyhawk fighters and a Liberator bomber had just departed Darwin, and the Australian duty officer assumed this was the same formation so the warnings were not acted upon. Anti-aircraft fire when it came was intense but largely ineffectual, and a second wave of 54 more planes struck at noon. The two attacks resulted in a greater number of bombs falling on Darwin than were dropped on Pearl Harbor, killing 243 people, wounding 400, and destroying 23 planes and eight ships. A memorial ceremony is held every year on 19 February at the Cenotaph in Darwin, starting at 09:58, the precise time of the first attack.

☆ FIRST Japanese attack on US mainland

Ellwood oil field, Santa Barbara, California. Second World War. 19:07 Monday 23 February 1942

From 19:07 until 19:45 the US mainland was bombarded by approximately 25 shells from a 5.5-inch deck gun aboard the Japanese submarine I-17, commanded by Kozo Nishino. Fortunately the damage was minimal: one man was wounded trying to defuse an unexploded shell and one oil rig needed superficial repairs. The submarine escaped unharmed. Although the raid was militarily insignificant, leading only to the tightening of American coastal defences, it was personally significant for Nishino. In the late 1930s he had commanded a Japanese tanker delivering crude oil to the Ellwood oil plant and on arrival he'd had to attend a formal greeting ceremony. While walking from the beach he slipped and fell into a prickly pear cactus and the rig workers roared with laughter at the sight of the dignified Nishino having cactus spines removed from his bottom. From then on he was a time bomb waiting for revenge – it took a world war and a historic first to secure it.

❑ ONLY animal to have been an official Japanese prisoner of war in the Second World War

Judy, No 81A, Medan. Second World War. Tuesday 10 March 1942

Shudi – Chinese for peaceful – was a pedigree pointer bitch born in Shanghai in 1927, whose name was changed to Judy when she was presented to the Royal Navy as a mascot. After a few postings she became the mascot of HMS *Grasshopper*, and on 14 February 1942 the *Grasshopper* was bombed and sunk en route to Java. A small group of survivors, including Judy, managed to get to a small uninhabited island where they survived after Judy discovered the island's only source of fresh water. After a few days the seven survivors commandeered a passing Chinese junk to take them to the north-east coast of Sumatra, where they began a 200-mile trek to reach the safety of Padang. But on 10 March their luck ran out; they were captured and spent two years in Medan prisoner of war camp. After Leading Aircraftsman Frank Williams shared his tiny ration of rice with her, Judy never left his side, earning her keep by warning unwary prisoners of poisonous snakes, scorpions, alligators and tigers. She also made friends with Camp Commandant Banno's local girlfriend, who ultimately saved Judy's life. While out on one of her forays Judy met a handsome stranger – a liaison which became apparent well before she gave birth to nine pups. Williams gave one of the pups to Banno's girlfriend and in return asked that Judy be made an official prisoner of war. Banno was sympathetic but said he wouldn't be able to explain the addition of an extra number of his list, so Williams suggested Banno add the suffix 'A' to Williams's own number, making her 'Judy 81A Medan'. She spent her time chasing monkeys, was scarred for life after attacking a crocodile, and on one occasion, after discovering the shin-bone of a elephant, spent two hours digging a hole big enough to bury it. On 25 June 1943 many prisoners, including Williams and Judy, were shipped from Sumatra to Singapore but the following day the ship was torpedoed. Williams survived, and believed Judy was dead until they were reunited three days later. They were recaptured and moved from camp to camp until the end of the war, when Williams smuggled Judy aboard the troopship returning prisoners to England. When newspapers told her story Judy became a national hero and in May 1946, with Williams at her side, the People's Dispensary for Sick Animals (PDSA) awarded her the Dickin Medal (the animal equivalent of the VC) 'For magnificent courage and endurance in Japanese prison camps, which helped to maintain morale among her fellow prisoners and also for saving many lives through her intelligence and watchfulness.' In 1948 she and Williams moved to East Africa, where Judy died at 17:00 on 17 February 1950. She was buried in the Royal Air Force jacket she had proudly worn as guest star of Crufts Dog Show.

* LAST day of the Bataan Death March

Camp O'Donnell concentration camp, Tarlac, Phillipine Islands. Second World War. Friday 24 April 1942

The greatest mass surrender in American military history occurred on 9 April 1942, when 75,000 Filipino and US soldiers, commanded by Major General Edward 'Ned' P King, formally surrendered to a Japanese army of 50,000 men under Lieutenant General Masaharu Homma. Just under half were starving, dehydrated, stricken with malaria or suffering from dysentery after months blockaded within the last US stronghold on the Bataan Peninsula in the Phillipines. The following day the infamous death march began, from Mariveles to San Fernando, some sixty miles away, from where the survivors would be moved onward by train (many of them dying of suffocation in the crowded boxcars) before marching the last eight miles to the notorious Camp O'Donnell. Prisoners were forced to march in the blistering sun without any shade, helmets, or water. Any troops who fell behind were executed or left to die, and anyone who dared ask for water was executed. Rare food rations invariably consisted of a handful of contaminated rice. It took the prisoners six days to reach San Fernando, during which more than 12,000 of them died. On 24 April the last survivors arrived at Camp O'Donnell, where several thousand more would die during their incarceration: by April 1945, when General MacArthur liberated the Phillipines, over a third of the prisoners who had survived the march had either died of disease or been killed by the Japanese. General Homma, who turned a blind eye to the atrocities inflicted on the prisoners, was executed for war crimes on 3 April 1946.

☆ FIRST major naval battle in which neither side sighted the other

Battle of the Coral Sea, Pacific Ocean between Australia and New Caledonia. Second World War. Monday 4 May 1942

The Battle of the Coral Sea was a sea battle fought entirely by air power. The Japanese Carrier Striking Force, under the command of Vice Admiral Takeo Takagi, converged on Port Moresby, New Guinea. US Navy Task Force 17, commanded by Rear Admiral Frank J Fletcher, was given the job of ridding the Pacific of the Japanese menace. The American and Japanese planes took off from carriers 180 miles apart before fighting the engagement, in which the Japanese lost 39 ships and many aircraft. Although the Americans lost the aircraft carrier *Lexington*, and the carrier *Yorktown* was severely damaged, the result was a strategic victory for the USA. During the whole battle, which lasted four days, until 8 May, no surface ship from either side sighted an enemy ship.

❏ ONLY British soldiers executed for mutiny during the Second World War

Gratien Fernando, C A Gauder and G B de Silva, Ceylon (now Sri Lanka). Second World War. August 1942

On the night of 8/9 May 1942 Ceylonese gunners of the Ceylon Garrison Artillery on Horsburgh Island attacked their British officers, yelling 'Asia for the Asiatics'. The rebel gunners wanted to hand the outpost over to the invading Japanese but instead the British managed to crush the rebellion and the three ringleaders were identified and hanged, Fernando on 4 August, Gauder on 7 August and de Silva on 8 August.

❏ ONLY sex symbol to invent a military weapon

Hedy Lamarr, US Patent 2,292,387 granted Tuesday 11 August 1942

Lamarr, born Hedwig Eva Maria Kiesler, was an Austrian-American actress who appeared in several early European films, including *Ecstasy* (1933), which included frequent nudity and was the first theatrical film to show sexual intercourse and female orgasm (by close-ups of Lamarr's face in passion). In 1933 she married arms manufacturer Fritz Mandal – the first of six husbands – and became a society hostess in Vienna, entertaining many foreign leaders including Hitler and Mussolini. Although Mandal specialised in shells and grenades, he also manufactured military aircraft and did extensive research into control systems. Lamarr obviously learned much from him. She moved to America where, at the height of her Hollywood fame, she developed the concept of 'frequency hopping' as a technique for controlling torpedoes by radio. Her co-inventor was her Hollywood neighbour George Antheil, a multi-talented composer and student of glandular endocrinology – Lamarr wanted to discuss how using glands could enlarge her world-famous breasts but the conservation turned instead to frequency hopping. Lamarr's idea was that the speed and unpredictability of the frequency changes would make control signals resistant to jamming or detection but she had not solved the problem of how to synchronise such rapid changes. Antheil suggested synchronising them in the same way he had co-ordinated the sixteen synchronised player pianos in his revolutionary *Ballet Méanique*. Together they developed a 'Secret

Communication System' using slotted paper rolls (similar to player-piano rolls) to synchronise the frequency changes in both transmitter and receiver, utilising exactly 88 frequencies, the number of keys on a piano. Their patent specified that a high-altitude observation plane could steer the torpedo from above but the navy rejected the idea, concluding that the mechanism would be too bulky to fit into a torpedo despite Antheil's insistence that it could be made small enough to squeeze into a watch. The idea was ahead of its time but in 1957 it was rediscovered by engineers who, using electronics rather than piano rolls, used it to develop a basic tool for secure military communications, and in 1962, three years after Lamarr's patent expired, it was installed on ships sent to blockade Cuba. Lamarr's concept lies behind nearly all today's anti-jamming devices, including the US government's Milstar defence communication satellite system, and in devices ranging from cordless telephones to Wi-Fi Internet connections. Neither Lamarr nor Antheil made any money from their patent but in 1997 the Electronic Frontier Foundation gave Lamarr a special, much overdue, award for her invention.

☆ FIRST land victory of the Second World War over the seemingly invincible Japanese

Battle of Milne Bay, New Guinea. Second World War. Saturday 5 September 1942

The Battle of Milne Bay, one of the great turning points of the war in the Pacific, began on the eastern tip of New Guinea on 25 August 1942. Two thousand four hundred Japanese marines, known as Special Naval Landing Forces, attacked Allied forces commanded by Australian Major General Cyril Clowes, who were defending three strategically-important airstrips. There were 8,824 Allied troops but only about 4,500 of them were infantry, and the Japanese enjoyed a significant advantage in the form of light tanks; the Japanese also had complete control of the sea at night, allowing reinforcement and supply, although this maritime advantage was offset by the Royal Australian Air Force's Nos 75 and 76 Squadrons, which played a critical role in the fierce fighting. The most common weapon used in the eleven-day battle was the bayonet, while the Japanese also employed jungle snipers and deception techniques such as calling out orders in English during the hours of darkness, often deceiving the Australians into betraying their positions. A turning point came when Australian troops discovered the bodies of comrades who had been taken prisoner tied to trees and stabbed full of holes – they had been used for bayonet practice. After that the Australians took no more prisoners. The Japanese retaliated by lying amongst the dead corpses and rising up to shoot the Australians, and it became regular practice for both sides to bayonet every dead body to ensure it was dead. The Japanese finally pulled out of Milne Bay on 5 September having lost more than half of their landing force, with just 1,320 troops evacuated. The Australians suffered 373 casualties, including 167 killed in action. None of the 39 Australians captured in the fighting survived, all having been tortured and killed. Just as important as the strategic victory was the fact that, thanks to the Australians, the myth of Japanese invulnerability was shattered – the Aussies had inflicted on the Japanese their first defeat on land, and the impact on Allied morale was inestimable.

DID YOU KNOW?

The Royal Australian Air Force, so vital to the victory at Milne Bay, was formed in 1921. During the First World War Australia was the only British Dominion with its own air force: the Australian Flying Corps. The AFC was replaced by the Australian Air-Corps in 1919 and then, on 31 March 1921, by the Australian Air Force, which received its Royal prefix five months later.

❏ **ONLY** US soldier to win the Bronze Star and the Purple Heart at the age of twelve

Calvin Graham, Battle of Guadalcanal. Second World War. Thursday 12 November 1942

Graham, who was born on 3 April 1930, lied about his age in order to enlist in the US Navy after the Japanese attack on Pearl Harbor, and at twelve years old, he became the youngest person ever to enlist in the US Navy. Still twelve, he was awarded the Bronze Star for his bravery in controlling fires aboard USS *South Dakota* during the Battle of Guadalcanal (*see following entry*) and the Purple Heart for shrapnel wounds to the jaw and mouth sustained during the battle. However, when his mother later revealed his true age he was imprisoned, dishonourably discharged, and stripped of his medals – all for lying about his age in order to serve his country. In 1978, after fighting to clear his name, his discharge was amended to 'honourable' and his Bronze Star reinstated. His Purple Heart was not reinstated until 1994, nearly two years after his death. Graham's story was dramatised in the 1988 film *Too Young the Hero*, in which he was played by Rick Schroder.

❏ **ONLY** US sea battle in which five brothers were killed
☆ **FIRST** US warships named after more than one person

George, Frank (Francis), Joe (Joseph), Matt (Madison) and Al (Albert) Sullivan, USS Juneau, Battle of Guadalcanal. Second World War. Friday 13 November 1942

The Sullivan brothers, from Waterloo, Iowa, all enlisted in the US Navy on 3 January 1942 on condition that serve together. The navy, which usually separated siblings, acceded to the Sullivans' request, with tragic consequences. The brothers, who ranged in age from

George, 27, to Al, nineteen, all died aboard the light cruiser USS *Juneau* during the Guadalcanal campaign, the first major US counter-offensive of the war in the Pacific. In August 1942 US Marines captured part of the island of Guadalcanal from the Japanese but the struggle for complete control was to continue for months. On 12 November air reconnaissance supporting a US supply convoy located a much larger Japanese supply convoy heading for the island, and at 01:45 on 13 November the warships escorting the two convoys engaged in the Battle of Guadalcanal. *Juneau* was badly damaged by a torpedo and later that day, while leaving the area, was hit and sunk by a second torpedo, this one from submarine I-26. Several days later a handful of survivors were picked up and reported that Frank, Joe, and Matt went down with the ship, Al drowned the next day, and George died several days later. Partly as a result of the Sullivans' deaths the US Navy adopted its Sole Survivor Policy to prevent a similar tragedy occurring again. The Navy also named two destroyers *The Sullivans* in honour of the brothers. The first was named in April 1943 by the brothers' mother, becoming the first US warship to be named after more than one person, and the second in 1995 by Al's granddaughter; Al's son James served aboard the first. The motto of both ships could have been the brothers' own: 'We stick together'.

DID YOU KNOW?

Each branch of the US military adopted its own policy regarding separation of siblings and protection of survivors if a sibling was killed; the case of the Niland brothers, US Army, inspired the feature film *Saving Private Ryan*. The Sullivans' own case was dramatised in the 1944 feature film *The Sullivans* (later renamed *The Fighting Sullivans*). The brothers are also commemorated by a convention centre, a street and a public park named after them in their hometown of Waterloo, Iowa.

❏ ONLY attempt to use bats as bombs

California, USA. Second World War. Saturday 15 May 1943

Operation X Ray was intended to drop millions of tiny bats over Tokyo armed with incendiary napalm charges, the plan being that when the bats went to roost millions of fires would destroy the wood and paper buildings peculiar to Japan. Bat bomb researchers risked their lives 'recruiting' perfect kamikaze bats but the plan – the brainchild of Pennsylvanian dentist Dr Lytle E Adams – suffered several setbacks and was suspended after several trials during which one batch of armed bats escaped and destroyed two aircraft hangars and a general's car. However, when all the data was collated it was estimated that while six clusters of conventional incendiary bombs would ignite about 160 fires, the same weight of bat bombs would start 4,768 fires. And so a memo was issued on 10 February 1944 ordering a final test and the preparation of one million incendiary capsules for the first full bat invasion of Japan, set for early autumn 1944. Then, after several technical delays for unspecified reasons, the whole operation was cancelled. The dejected Dr Adams later invented a vending machine for fried chicken but that, too, was rejected.

☆ FIRST US Soldier's Medal awarded to a woman

Edith Greenwood. Monday 21 June 1943

The Soldier's Medal, introduced by Congress on 2 July 1926, is awarded to any person serving with or alongside the US Army who displays 'heroism not involving actual conflict with an enemy'. The first woman to receive the medal was Nurse Edith Greenwood, who repeatedly risked her life to save her patients after fire broke out in a station hospital near Yuma, Arizona, on 17 April 1943.

❏ **ONLY** VC awarded solely on evidence given by the enemy

Flying Officer Lloyd Allan Trigg, Royal New Zealand Air Force, serving with the 200 Squadron, RAF, Atlantic Ocean, 240 miles south-west of Dakar, Senegal, Africa. Second World War. 09:45 Wednesday 11 August 1943

On 11 August 1943 Trigg, the captain and pilot of a Liberator bomber, spotted a surfaced U-boat, the U-468, which was captained by Oberleutnant zur See Clemens Schamong on his first command. Trigg immediately attacked but his plane burst into flames during the approach after receiving numerous hits from the U-boat's two 20mm cannons. Trigg could have broken off the engagement and made a forced landing in the ocean but instead he continued the attack and released six depth charges from a height of just 50 feet, two of which exploded within six feet of U-468's hull, causing catastrophic damage. Trigg's plane then hit the sea 300 yards from the U-boat and exploded on impact. U468 sank within ten minutes. Some twenty crew-members managed to jump overboard but many of them died of their injuries while in the water or were killed by sharks. Seven survivors, including Schamong, managed to keep predatory fish away by ducking their heads underwater and 'roaring'. Then one of the sailors found a rubber dinghy that had broken loose from the Liberator and the seven survivors clambered aboard. The next day an RAF plane spotted the dinghy and guided HMS *Clakia* to rescue the men. None of the prisoners would reveal any details of their operation but they all, without reserve, declared their unmitigated admiration for the courage of Trigg and his crew. With none but the enemy as witnesses to Trigg's courage it was, uniquely, on their testimony that he was posthumously awarded the VC.

❏ ONLY animal to be awarded the Distinguished Service Cross

Chips. Second World War. Sunday 24 October 1943

Under General Order No 79 of the 3rd Infantry Division, Major General Lucien Truscott proudly conferred the Distinguished Service Cross on Chips – a shepherd-husky cross – for 'courageous action in single-handedly eliminating a dangerous machine-gun nest and causing surrender of crew'. But on 19 January 1944 the US War Department prohibited the awarding of decorations to animals and sadly, on 3 February 1944, Chips's award was rescinded.

❏ ONLY military operation successfully undertaken by a man who never was

Major Martin, off the coast Huelva, Spain. Second World War. 04:30 Sunday 30 April 1944

'The most successful strategic deception in the history of warfare' was achieved by a man who never was, and resulted in British Naval Intelligence convincing Hitler that the planned Allied landings in southern Europe would take place in Greece and Sardinia rather than the intended location of Sicily. Codenamed Operation Mincemeat, the plan was the brainchild of Flight Lieutenant Charles Cholmondeley of MI5 and top Naval Intelligence officer Lieutenant Commander Ewen Montagu. The idea was simple – plant false information on a corpse to make it more credible – but the planning and execution were more complex. They couldn't drop the body on land and make it look as if the man had died due to an unopened parachute because the Germans knew that the Allies would never allow sensitive documents to be taken over enemy territory. Instead they made him appear to be a victim of a plane crash at sea, and then set about creating the fictitious Major Martin. With the aid of pathologist Bentley Purchase they secured the corpse of a 34-year-old man who had recently died of chemically-induced pneumonia as the result of ingesting rat poison, knowing that the fluid in his lungs would be consistent with drowning. The family of the dead man agreed on the condition that the man's real identity would never be revealed. The next step was to bring the corpse to life. They named him Captain/Acting Major William Martin, Royal Marines, born 1907, in Cardiff, Wales, and assigned to Headquarters, Combined Operations. Making Martin an acting major would give the impression that he was a trusted officer. Martin was engaged to Pam – actually a clerk at MI5 – and carried her photograph and love letters, plus an ill-tempered letter from his father expressing his displeasure with his son's choice of bride. They also provided a set of keys, theatre stubs for a 22 April performance, a statement from his club for lodging in London, overdue bills, a new identification card to replace one supposedly lost, an expired pass to Combined Operations HQ that he forgot to renew, and an complaint from his bank manager regarding his overdraft of £17 19s 11d. Also among the documents was a master-stroke of reverse psychology. One letter disclosed that deception plans were being drawn up to convince the Germans that the Allies were going to invade Sicily! Martin would be wearing a type of lock and chain device used by bank couriers, attaching him to the briefcase containing all the military plans. After being preserved in dry ice in a London mortuary the corpse was taken in a sealed steel canister to the submarine HMS *Seraph* in Holy Loch, Scotland, and then to southern Spain where it was put into the sea at 04:30 on 30 April some 1,600 yards from shore near the town of Huelva. Spain, despite being officially neutral, was sympathetic to the Axis and Huelva was home to the well-known Nazi agent Adolf Clauss, the son of the German consul, who operated under the cover of an agriculture technician. The body was discovered around 09:30 by local fishermen. The local authorities handed over the false documents to Clauss, who teased open the sealed letters, photographed the entire contents then resealed everything. While the photographic evidence was rushed to Berlin to be evaluated, a post-mortem reported that Martin had fallen into the sea while still alive, presumably the victim of a plane crash, that death was due to drowning, and that the body had been in the sea between three and five days. When the British Vice-Consul, F K Hazeldene, demanded the return of the documents the Spanish returned them 'unopened', and after the body was returned Major Martin was buried with full military honours on 4 May in Huelva. The plan paid off – Montagu established that their ploy reached at least as high as Admiral Canaris, head of the Abwehr, and that apparently Hitler himself was so convinced that the bogus documents were genuine that he ordered the reinforcement of Sardinia and Corsica, sent Rommel to Athens to form an Army Group, and diverted patrol boats, minesweepers and minelayers earmarked for the defence of Sicily. Operation Mincemeat had been swallowed whole – when the Allies invaded on 9 July they met relatively little resistance and the conquest of Sicily took just one month.

DID YOU KNOW?

In 1988 it was suggested that 'Major Martin' was a Welsh gardener named Emlyn Howells, who died of tuberculosis on 6 January 1943, and in 1996 that he was a vagrant Welsh alcoholic named Glyndwr Michael, who died of ingesting rat poison on 28 January 1943. However, new theories suggest that he could have been one of two sailors killed aboard the aircraft carrier HMS *Dasher* when it blew up in the Clyde Estuary on 27 March 1943 – either John 'Jack' Meville or the coincidentally (?) named Tom Martin. Whoever he was, his corpse saved countless lives.

☆ FIRST V1 attack on England
☆ FIRST V1 to hit London
☆ FIRST fatalities caused by a V1 attack

Grove Road, Bethnal Green, London. Second World War. 04:25 Tuesday 13 June 1944

On 13 June 1944 the Germans launched the first ten V1 rockets against England. These pilotless, jet-propelled aircraft were twenty-five feet four and a half inches long, made of sheet steel and plywood, and could carry 1,874 pounds of high explosive at a speed of 350mph for about 130 miles. It took about twenty to twenty-five minutes for the V1 to run out of fuel, and after the engine stopped there would a nerve-wracking twelve second wait for the rocket to hit the ground and explode. Five of the V1s (which stood for *Vergeltungswaffe Eins*, or 'Vengeance Weapon One') crash-landed near their take-off site in Watten, France; one went missing, presumed to have crashed into the English Channel, and four reached England. Three of these four fell short of their target, landing with no casualties at Swanscombe, Kent, at 04:13; Cuckfield, Sussex, at 04:20; and Platt, near Sevenoaks, Kent, at 05:06. Only one reached London, striking Grove Road at 04:25, killing six people, seriously injuring thirty and leaving 200 homeless. The first fatalities were: Dora Cohen (55), Connie Day (32), Willie Rogers (50), Lennie Sherman (12), and Ellen Woodcraft (19) and her eight-month-old baby, Tom. Small comfort was offered when it was revealed that a Messerschmitt 410, believed to have been the official observer, was shot down just east of Choats Manor Way, Barking Marshes. The wireless operator was killed after bailing out too low for his parachute to open and the pilot was killed on impact. Londoners called the V1s 'flying bombs', 'buzz bombs' or 'doodlebugs'.

☆ FIRST jet fighter to engage an enemy in combat
☆ FIRST jet bomber
☆ FIRST jet fighter to be shot down

Messerschmitt Me 262A. Second World War. Tuesday 25 July 1944

The jet engine was invented by British aeronautical engineer Frank Whittle and patented in 1930. But the first jet engine into the air was invented independently by German engineer Hans von Ohain, patented in 1934 and first flew in August 1939. Unfortunately for Whittle, lack of money or encouragement meant that he was not able to demonstrate the world's first jet engine – which he did on the ground – until 12 April 1937, and Britain's first jet aircraft, a Gloster-Whittle E.28/39 piloted by Flight Lieutenant Gerry Sayer, didn't take to the air until 15 May 1941. Meanwhile in Germany, on 24 August 1939, a Heinkel He 178 piloted by Flugkapitän Erich Warsitz made the first ever flight by a jet-powered aircraft – followed three days later by an official demonstration which is often erroneously described as the first jet flight. The Germans also won the race for the first jet fighter: a prototype Messerschmitt Me 262A piloted by Fritz Wendel made its maiden flight on 18 July 1942, and the production model went into service in June 1944, becoming the first jet aircraft to engage an enemy in combat when it intercepted an RAF Mosquito over Munich on 25 July 1944 – the RAF pilot, Flight Lieutenant Wall, evaded the jet and escaped into a bank of clouds. The Me 262 also had the honour of being the first jet bomber – a modified version known as the Me 262A-2 Sturmvogel ('Stormbird') was evaluated in June 1944 – and the dubious honour of being the first jet fighter to be shot down: two Me 262A-1a fighters were shot down on or about 10 October 1944 by P-51D Mustang escort fighters of the 361st Fighter Group, US 8th Air Force.

❑ ONLY Allied jet aircraft to see active service in the Second World War

Gloster Meteor. Thursday 27 July 1944

The Gloster Meteor – descended from Britain's first jet aeroplane, the Gloster-Whittle E.28/39 (*see previous entry*) – was first flown on 5 March 1943 from RAF Cranwell by Michael Daunt, and went into service with 616 Squadron that July. The Meteor was first flown in a combat mission on 27 July 1944, just two days after a German Messerschmitt became the first jet fighter to engage an enemy aircraft (*see previous entry*). The Meteor's first mission – to intercept V1 flying rockets – was unsuccessful due to problems with the plane's guns, but its first success came just over a week later on 4 August without the use of guns. The first RAF jet pilot to score a 'kill' was Flying Officer 'Dixie' Dean of 616 Squadron who, his guns having jammed, flew alongside a V1 flying bomb and used the wing of his Meteor to tip the missile, making it crash into the ground.

❑ ONLY member of the British army to receive the Military Medal three times in the Second World War

Sergeant Fred 'Buck' Kite, Le Grand Bonfait, France. Second World War. Thursday 3 August 1944

Kite joined the 3rd Royal Tank Regiment in 1938, at the age of 17. He won his first Military Medal for bravery in January 1943, three miles west of Tahuna in North Africa, when he 'excelled himself' while engaged on a special 'desperately difficult' reconnaissance mission. His second Military Medal (or first Bar) was awarded for leadership, initiative and personal courage during action near the village of Bras, Normandy, in July 1944.

When his squadron was pinned down by two enemy tanks and two 88mm guns he refused to surrender and managed to disable the first Mark IV tank and one of the 88mm guns, thus holding the position and allowing his comrades to advance in safety. His third Military Medal (or second Bar) was awarded for the 'greatest personal courage and his example of remaining in action against odds that were much against him' at Le Grand Bonfait, Normandy, on 3 August 1944. Kite was commanding one of several tanks on the edge of an orchard. All the other tanks in his unit were out of action but he nonetheless managed to hold his position even when attacked by at least one Tiger and four Panther tanks, making at least five direct hits on enemy tanks before he was hit himself and seriously wounded. Viscount Montgomery's signature appeared on all three of Kite's medal citations, first as General Officer Commanding Eighth Army, then as Commander-in-Chief 21st Army Group, and finally as Field Marshal. Kite went on to see action in Egypt, Crete and Greece, rising to the rank of Sergeant, and after the war one of the great British heroes became chief wages clerk in a factory. He died in June 1993 at the age of 72.

❑ ONLY US president to have been shot down as a military pilot

George Herbert Walker Bush, Chi-Chi Jima, Pacific Ocean. Second World War. 08:15 Saturday 2 September 1944

George Bush Snr joined the US Navy on his eighteenth birthday, and when he received his wings on 9 June 1943, just three days before his nineteenth birthday, he became the Navy's youngest aviator. Assigned to a torpedo squadron operating from the carrier USS *San Jacinto* in the Pacific, Bush flew the Grumman TBM Avenger – a bomber so slow that airmen said it could fall faster than it could fly. At 07:15 on 2 September 1944 Bush took off as one of four pilots detailed to bomb Japanese gun emplacements on the island Chi-Chi Jima, close to the legendary Iwo Jima. His crew consisted of radio operator and tail gunner Jack Delaney, and family friend Ted White, who stood in as turret gunner at the last moment; his plane had 'Barbara' painted on the side in honour of his fiancée, Barbara Pierce. While making his diving attack at about 08:15 Bush's plane was hit by the intense anti-aircraft fire and his engine caught fire, filling the cockpit with smoke. Despite the fire, which Bush could see edging towards the fuel tanks, he completed his dive and released four 500-pound bombs directly on target. He turned back over the sea and ordered Delaney and White to bale out. He then baled out himself but (probably due to pulling the ripcord too soon) first his head then the parachute canopy struck the tail of the plane – miraculously the only damage was a gashed forehead and a small tear in the canopy which made him fall fast but still safely. After hitting the water he was stung by jellyfish before climbing aboard the emergency life raft and starting to drift back towards Japanese-held Chi-Chi Jima. Luckily, after nearly four hours, he was rescued by the lifeguard submarine USS *Finback* but he later learned that neither Delaney nor White had survived – one went down with the plane and the other was seen jumping but his parachute failed to open. For this action Bush received the Distinguished Flying Cross.

DID YOU KNOW?

In total Bush flew fifty-eight combat missions, for which he received the Distinguished Flying Cross, three Air Medals, and the Presidential Unit Citation. He returned home on Christmas Eve 1944 and two weeks later, on 6 January 1945, he married Barbara, who went on to become America's First Lady.

❑ ONLY Second World War soldier to capture an entire village on his own

James I Spurrier Jr, Achain, France. Second World War. 14:00 Tuesday 14 November 1944

When Spurrier enlisted in the US Army in September 1940 he wrote his name in the wrong blanks and became officially 'Junior J Spurrier'. He proved to be a fine soldier and earned the Distinguished Service Cross after spearheading an assault on a stubbornly defended hill position near Lay St. Christopher, France – riding a tank and firing a .50-calibre machine gun, he killed more than a dozen Germans and captured 22 others. But his finest hour came after being promoted staff sergeant – on 13 November 1944, Spurrier earned America's highest military decoration, the Medal of Honor, for single-handedly capturing the village of Achain. His Medal of Honor citation reads:

> For conspicuous gallantry and intrepidity at risk of his life above and beyond the call of duty in action against the enemy at Achain, France, on 13 November 1944. At 2 p.m., Company G attacked the village of Achain from the east. S/Sgt. Spurrier armed with a BAR passed around the village and advanced alone. Attacking from the west, he immediately killed 3 Germans. From this time until dark, S/Sgt. Spurrier, using at different times his BAR and M1 rifle, American and German rocket launchers, a German automatic pistol, and handgrenades, continued his solitary attack against the enemy regardless of all types of small-arms and automatic-weapons fire. As a result of his heroic actions he killed an officer and 24 enlisted men and captured 2 officers and 2 enlisted men. His valor has shed fresh honor on the U.S. Armed Forces.

✱ LAST American soldier shot for desertion
❑ ONLY American deserter executed in the Second World War

Private Edward Donald 'Eddie' Slovik, 86 Rue de General Dourgeois, Ste-Marie-aux-Mines, France. Second World War. 10:05 Wednesday 31 January 1945

Slovik's criminal record for breaking and entering, then stealing and crashing a car while on parole, originally made him unfit for military duty but he was later reclassified and drafted by the US Army. On 20 August 1944 he was one of twelve reinforcements assigned to Company G, 109th Infantry Regiment, US 28th Infantry Division. While travelling to his unit in France he and Private John Tankey got separated from the others and the next morning they found a non-combat Canadian unit and remained with them for the next six weeks. Eventually Tankey wrote to their regiment explaining their absence before he and Slovik reported for duty on 7 October. No charges against them were filed but the following day Slovik informed his company commander, Captain Ralph Grotte, that he was 'too scared' to serve in a rifle company and asked to be re-assigned to a rear area unit, threatening to desert if assigned to a rifle unit. His request was refused and the next day Slovik gave a note to a military policeman stating his intention to 'run away' if he were sent into combat. His commanding officer, Lieutenant-Colonel Ross Henbest, gave him the chance to tear up the note and face no further charges but Slovik refused and wrote a further note stating he understood what he was doing and its consequences. He was confined in the stockade until divisional judge advocate, Lieutenant-Colonel Henry Summer, again offered Slovik an opportunity to rejoin his unit and have the charges against him suspended. He also offered Slovik a transfer to another infantry regiment. Slovik declined these offers, saying, 'I've made up my mind. I'll take my court martial.' With desertion rates increasing it was decided to make an example of Slovik. He was charged with desertion to avoid hazardous duty and court martialled on 11 November 1944. The nine officers of the court found Slovik guilty and sentenced him to death. A personal letter pleading for mercy to Supreme Allied Commander Dwight D Eisenhower – which Slovik began by misspelling his name 'Dear General Eisenhowser' – was rejected. In fact Eisenhower never even read the letter. The US military, not wanting to alert the French that they were dealing with desertion problems so drastically, selected a high-walled garden on the northern outskirts of the village for the execution. As the guns used were M-1 rifles, which can kill a man at two miles, there was serious risk of ricochet at twenty paces – a risk diminished by carpenters building a six-foot square double-boarded back wall. When the firing squad arrived Slovik was already tied to a post in front of the back board, wearing a black hood over his head. His last words were to the priest Father Cummings who said to him, 'Eddie when you get Up There, say a little prayer for me.' Slovik replied, 'Okay, Father. I'll pray that you don't follow me too soon.' At 10:05 the twelve-man firing squad faced 24-year-old Slovik, eleven of the guns loaded with live bullets. Not one of the bullets struck his heart. They ranged from high in his neck, out to the left shoulder, over the left chest, under the heart and one bullet entered his left upper arm. Slovik slumped forward and everyone saw him struggle up at least twice. After the first volley his heart was still beating and orders were given for the firing squad to reload, at which point the chaplain turned to the officer in charge and said, 'Give him another volley if you like it so much.' Fortunately by the time they were ready Slovik was pronounced dead. He was buried in Plot E of Oise-Aisne Cemetery in Fère-en-Tardenois, alongside 96 other American soldiers executed for crimes such as murder and rape. In 1987, 42 years after his execution, Slovik's remains were returned to Michigan and reburied in Woodmere Cemetery, Detroit, next to his wife Antoinette, who had died in 1979. Although more than 21,000 soldiers were given varying sentences for desertion during the Second World War – including 49 death sentences – only Slovik's death sentence was carried out.

DID YOU KNOW?

The idea of giving one member of the firing squad a blank, in order to leave everyone with reasonable doubt as to whether they had actually played a part in killing Slovik, was a complete waste of time. The high-powered M-1 rifle kicks like a mule when a live round is fired and there is almost no recoil when a blank is fired; moreover it automatically elects a shell of a live round but will not eject a blank. Everyone who fired a live round would have known that they directly participated in Slovik's death.

❏ ONLY fighter pilot to be imprisoned and decorated by his country for the same act

Mikhail Petrovich Devyatayev, Usedom Island Prison Camp. Second World War. Thursday 8 February 1945

Devyatayev was a Soviet fighter pilot best known for his amazing escape from a Nazi concentration camp on the island of Usedom in the Baltic Sea. Conscripted into the Red Army in 1938, he graduated from the Chkalov Flying School two years later and made his first kill on 24 June 1941, destroying a German Junkers Ju-87 just two days after Germany attacked the Soviet Union. On 13 July 1944 he was taken prisoner and held in the Lódz concentration camp after being shot down near Lvov, over German-held territory. On 13 August an unsuccessful escape attempt resulted in him being transferred to Sachsenhausen concentration camp, and from there he was transferred to Usedom to be a part of a forced labour crew working for the German missile programme in Peenemünde. On 8 February 1945 he managed to hijack a German Heinkel 111 H22 bomber and fly himself and nine other Soviet prisoners of war off the 'island of death', landing in Soviet-held territory despite being shot at by Soviet anti-aircraft defences. All ten escapees survived the landing but were almost killed by Soviet troops who, understandably, thought they were Germans. The Soviet authorities refused to believe Devyatayev's story, arguing that it would have been impossible to take over an aircraft without German cooperation. Then, even though the escapees provided important information about the German missile program, Devyatayev was accused of being a German spy and sent to a penal military unit from which he was not discharged until November 1945. Even then, with suspicions still rife, the only work he could obtain was manual labour in Kazan. It was twelve years before his name was finally cleared, after the personal intervention of Sergei Korolev, head of the Soviet space programme, who argued that the information provided by Devyatayev and the other escapees had been crucial for the Soviet space development. On 15 August 1957 Devyatayev became a Hero of the Soviet Union and was awarded the Order of Lenin, the Order of the Red Banner twice, the Order of the Patriotic War (first and second class), and many other awards. He continued to live in Kazan, working as a captain of the first-ever Russian hydrofoil passenger ships on the Volga. He died in Kazan on 24 November 2002 and was buried with full military honours in the Arskoe veteran memorial cemetery.

❑ ONLY British queen to have volunteered for military service

(Princess) Elizabeth, Auxiliary Territorial Service (ATS), Aldershot Barracks. Second World War. Saturday 24 February 1945

In February 1945 George VI finally gave way to his eighteen-year-old daughter's persistent request to be allowed to 'join up' and 'do her bit' for the war effort. Her sister Margaret was jealous but Elizabeth dismissed her envy, saying, 'Margaret always wants what I've got.' Elizabeth signed on for the Auxiliary Territorial Service as 'No. 230873 Second Subaltern Elizabeth Alexandra Mary Windsor. Age 18. Eyes: Blue. Hair: Brown. Height 5' 3".' She enrolled on a three-week NCOs' cadre course at Aldershot Barracks and was required to learn vehicle maintenance, map reading, driving in convoy and stripping and servicing an engine. Because Elizabeth had led a secluded life since the outbreak of war none of the other eleven women picked for the course knew in advance what she looked like, and one of the girls noted that she was 'Quite striking ... and she uses lipstick!' While the other NCOs slept in dormitory huts Elizabeth was chauffeured back home to Windsor Castle every evening and was allowed to lunch in the officers' mess. During her first practical lesson she was handed a spanner, and when asked if she had ever held one before she giggled and said, 'No! Never.' On the second evening she spent time excitedly explaining a car's ignition system to her father. The king and queen visited Elizabeth's depot to watch her take her final test, and were highly impressed to see her under a car with greasy hands, face and overalls looking 'very grave and determined to get good marks and do the right thing'. She passed with flying colours, and later proved her proficiency by driving her company commander from Aldershot to Buckingham Palace – taking an interesting route that included driving around Piccadilly Circus twice. On VE Day, 8 May 1945, she and Princess Margaret slipped out of Buckingham Palace and mingled unrecognised with the crowds, linking arms and singing and dancing, Elizabeth proudly wearing her ATS uniform.

* LAST bomb to fall on London during the Second World War

Hughes Mansions, Vallance Road, Bethnal Green. Second World War. 07:21 Tuesday 27 March 1945

By a tragic irony this incident, which occurred on the very last day of Hitler's V1-V2 campaign (*see following entry*), was the most devastating of all the rocket attacks on London's East End. The V2 rocket dropped in the middle of Hughes Mansions at 07:21, just as residents were getting ready for work, and the blast sheered away the interior walls, causing the building to collapse and killing 134 people.

DID YOU KNOW?

Notorious gangsters Ronnie and Reggie Kray lived at 178 Vallance Road (*previous entry*) which was nicknamed Fort Vallance. During the war this area of Vallance Road became known as 'Deserter's Corner' because so many locals deserted or ignored their call-up papers – including the twins' father, Charlie Kray Snr. In 1952, after being conscripted and reporting to the Royal Fusiliers at the nearby Tower of London, the twins went AWOL on their first day. They became serial deserters until they finally achieved their ambition in 1954 – a dishonourable discharge.

✴ **LAST** V2 rocket of the Second World War
✴ **LAST** British civilian casualty of the Second World War

Ivy Millichamp, Court Road/Kynaston Road, Orpington, Kent. Second World War. 16:54 Tuesday 27 March 1945

The last V2 rocket of the war caused tremendous damage and many injuries but resulted in only one fatality: 34-year-old Ivy Millichamp of 88 Kynaston Road. In 1989 a memorial tombstone was erected in her honour at the local All Saints churchyard.

✴ **LAST** public appearance of Adolf Hitler

Berlin, Germany. Friday 20 April 1945

On his 56th birthday, in a final desperate attempt to boost morale, Hitler came out of his Berlin bunker to be filmed presenting awards to twenty Hitler Youth soldiers, all war orphans, who had shown courage under Russian fire. It was to be Hitler's last appearance, and the last newsreel produced by Joseph Goebbels, the head of Nazi propaganda. The most remarkable award was that of the Iron Cross to twelve-year-old Alfred Zeck, who became the youngest recipient of the prestigious medal. Hitler then returned to the safety of his underground headquarters, leaving the boys to carry on the fight against the Russian tanks. He never left the bunker alive.

❑ **ONLY** US mainland fatalities of the Second World War

Lakeview, Oregon. Second World War. Saturday 5 May 1945

In 1945 the Japanese launched a number of unmanned high-altitude balloons armed with anti-personnel bombs and incendiary devices, hoping that the jet steam would carry them across to the western mainland of the United States. On 5 May 1945 the Reverend Archie Mitchell and his wife Elsie organised a picnic at Lakeview, Oregon, for five children: Edward Engen, Jay Gifford, Ethel Patzke, Richard Patzke and Sherman Shoemaker. In the woods one of the children discovered one of the Japanese balloons, known as *fusen bakuden*, meaning 'wind ship combs'. As the children dragged the balloon out of the woods it exploded, killing everyone except the minister. On 7 June 1949 Congress awarded Elsie Mitchell's husband $5,000 compensation and $3,000 dollars per child to the parents of the children. The site of the explosion is now called the Mitchell Recreational Centre. The Rev. Archie Mitchell became a missionary in Indochina where, in 1962, he was captured by Vietcong guerrillas and never seen again.

☆ FIRST atomic bomb used on an enemy

Hiroshima, Japan. Second World War, 08:15:40 Monday 6 August 1945

The $2 billion programme to develop the atom bomb – codenamed the 'Manhattan Project' – was launched in 1942 after Einstein advised US President Roosevelt that the Germans may be developing such a bomb. After the test detonation of the world's first atom bomb on 16 July 1945 the project's scientific director, J Robert Oppenheimer, quoted from a Hindu scripture: 'I am become death, destroyer of worlds'. Thirteen days later, on 29 July 1945, Japan rejected an ultimatum to surrender unconditionally or suffer 'complete destruction', so US President Truman authorised the immediate use of atomic force, reiterating the call for surrender and warning the Japanese of 'a rain of ruin from the air, the like of which has never been seen on this earth'. On 4 August American planes dropped leaflets over the city of Hiroshima warning the inhabitants that their city would be obliterated, and two days later the *Enola Gay* – a B-29 long-range bomber named after the mother of its pilot, Colonel Paul Warfield Tibbets Jnr – took off from the Mariana Islands to commit the awesome deed. At 08:15 bombardier Major Thomas W Ferebee released the bomb, nicknamed *Little Boy*, which fell for 40 seconds before exploding 1,890 feet above the centre of Hiroshima, vaporising the city, killing 80,000 people outright and condemning an estimated 100,000 more to slow, agonising deaths from radiation poisoning. The mushroom cloud rose to 60,000 feet. *Enola Gay*'s tail gunner, who witnessed the explosion from ten miles away as the plane returned to base, voiced a thought that would be echoed around the globe: 'My God. What have we done?'

☆ FIRST conscientious objector to be awarded the Medal of Honor

Private First Class Desmond T Doss, US Army Medical Detachment, 307th Infantry, 77th Infantry Division. Second World War. Friday 12 October 1945

The Medal of Honor is the highest military decoration awarded by the United States, popularly known as the Congressional Medal of Honor because the president presents it 'in the name of the Congress'. It is bestowed on a member of the US armed forces who distinguishes himself or herself '… conspicuously by gallantry and intrepidity at the risk of his life above and beyond the call of duty while engaged in an action against an enemy of the United States …' Twenty-six-year-old Doss was a Seventh Day Adventist whose religious beliefs barred him from carrying a weapon into conflict. Still wanting to serve his country he volunteered as a medic, in which capacity he was wounded twice, on Guam and Leyte, while tending the injured under heavy enemy fire. His Medal of Honor was awarded for numerous acts of extreme heroism during the Battle of Okinawa, which took place from 29 April to 21 May 1945.

On one occasion, ignoring orders to leave the area, he scaled a 400-foot jagged escarpment under a heavy concentration of artillery, mortar and machine gun fire and rescued 75 casualties, single-handedly lowering each man down to safety on a rope-supported litter. On another occasion Doss crawled to the mouth of a cave filled with Japanese snipers to administer plasma to a wounded GI, and on the same day he carried an injured soldier 100 yards to safety while continually exposed to enemy fire. On 21 May, while rendering aid to the wounded in exposed territory, he was seriously wounded in the leg by a grenade. Rather than risk the life of fellow medics he treated his own injuries and waited five hours before two litter bearers reached him and started carrying him to cover. Seeing a wounded soldier, Doss crawled off the litter and instructed the bearers to tend to the other soldier first. While awaiting their return he was hit again, suffering a compound fracture of the arm, so he bound a rifle stock to his arm as a splint and crawled the final 300 yards to safety. On 12 October President Harry S Truman personally presented Doss the Medal of Honor in a ceremony at the White House. Doss remained the only conscientious objector to receive the Medal of Honor until another army medic, Corporal Thomas W Bennett, was awarded it for his courage during the Vietnam War.

☆ **FIRST** Nazi war criminal to be hanged at Nuremberg
✳ **LAST** words of all ten Nazi war criminals to be hanged at Nuremberg

Joachim Von Ribbentrop, gymnasium of Nuremberg Prison. 01:11 Wednesday 16 October 1946

Twenty-four Nazi leaders were tried by the International Military Tribunal at Nuremberg. Twelve were sentenced to death but only ten were hanged because Martin Boorman had previously escaped and was tried *in absentia*, and Herman Goering committed suicide in the death cell by biting on a concealed cyanide capsule just two hours before he was due to be hanged. Three eight-foot high wooden scaffolds were prepared, two of them used alternately with the third as a reserve. The condemned were hanged individually but, to save time, the military police brought in each prisoner while the previous victim was still dangling at the end of the rope on the adjacent scaffold. The hangman was the incompetent, bungling US Major John Woods. The first to be hanged was von Ribbentrop, the former Ambassador to Britain and Hitler's last foreign minister, whose last words were:

> My last wish is that Germany realise its entity and that an
> understanding be reached between East and West. I wish
> peace to the world.

The bolt was pulled at 01:11 but, though he fell through the trap 'like a stone', it still took ten minutes for him to strangle to death. Second was Chief of Staff General Field Marshal Wilhelm von Keitel, 64, who ordered the killing of prisoners of war after an escape attempt. He was the first military leader to be executed under the new concept of international law which refused to accept the defence of carrying out the orders of superiors. His last words were:

> I call on God Almighty to have mercy on the German
> people. More than two million German soldiers went to
> their death for the Fatherland before me. I follow now
> my sons – all for Germany.

He took 24 minutes to die. Third was chief of the Reich main security office General Ernest Kaltenbrunner, 44, who dismissed the accusation of atrocities at concentration camps as Allied propaganda even though he had personally ordered the gassing of 3 million humans at Auschwitz. His last words were:

> I have loved my German people and my Fatherland with
> a warm heart. I have done my duty by the laws of my
> people and I am sorry this time my people were led by

> men who were not soldiers and that crimes were
> committed of which I had no knowledge. Germany,
> good luck.

Fourth was head of foreign affairs Alfred Rosenberg, 53, Hitler's early mentor and the guiding light behind the Nazi philosophy. When asked if he had any last words he said, 'No.' Fifth was former Governor-General of Poland Hans Frank, 46, who had converted to Roman Catholicism in prison and walked to the gallows smiling. His last words were:

> I am thankful for the kind treatment during my captivity
> and I ask God to accept me with mercy.

Sixth was Reich Minister of the Interior Wilhelm Frick, 69, who had been responsible for the anti-Semitic and concentration camp laws, whose last words were: 'Long live eternal Germany.' His nose was almost severed in the fall, either by hitting his head of the edge of the trap or by the rope being too loose. Seventh was the leading Jew-baiter Julius Streicher, 61, who, as he reached the scaffold, screamed: 'Heil Hitler!' Asked for his name he snarled:

> You know my name well. Julius Streicher! … Now it goes
> with God … Purim Fest 1946! (This is a reference to the
> Jewish holiday commemorating the execution of
> Haman, ancient persecutor of the Jews)… The
> Bolsheviks will hang you one day! … I am with God.
> Adele, my dear wife.

When the trap opened he dropped, kicking wildly, and was heard groaning until the hangman went inside and 'Something happened that put a stop to the groans and brought the rope to a standstill.' Eighth was head of the slave labour programme Fritz Sauckel, 51, whose last words were:

> I am dying innocent. The sentence is wrong. God protect
> Germany and make Germany great again. Long live
> Germany! God protect my family!

He died groaning at the end of the rope. Ninth was Chief of the

Operations Staff and Hitler's closest military adviser General Alfred Jodl, 56, whose last words were:

> My greetings to you, my Germany.

He took 18 minutes to die. Tenth and last was Reich Governor of Austria and Reich Commissioner of the Netherlands Artur Seyss-Inquart, 54, whose last words were:

> I hope that this execution is the last act of tragedy of the Second World War and that the lesson taken from this world war will be that peace and understanding should exist between peoples. I believe in Germany.

The trap swallowed him at 02:45. The ten executions had taken one hour and thirty-four minutes. All the bodies were laid out on the gymnasium floor, as was Goering's corpse, to show that he too had been symbolically hanged. The corpses were later taken to Dachau, near Munich, where with deliberate irony they were cremated in the ovens of the concentration camp. The ashes were then thrown into the River Isar.

☆ FIRST coining of the term 'Cold War'

Bernard Baruch, South Carolina, USA. Wednesday 16 April 1947

The phrase 'Cold War' means a state of distrust and mutual hostility between states that has not quite broken out into declared war. It was first publicly spoken in a speech written by Herbert Bayward Swope, former editor of *New York World*, and delivered by the American economist and presidential adviser Bernard Baruch before the South Carolina legislature. As US Ambassador to the United Nations Atomic Energy Commission, Baruch said, 'Let us not be deceived – we are today in the midst of a cold war.' Swope had used the term in the early 1940s in a personal letter to describe America's situation prior to Pearl Harbour. The Russians called it 'the pushbutton war'.

DID YOU KNOW?

Although Swope undoubtedly coined the phrase and Baruch put it into general currency, George Orwell used the term 'Cold War' in a newspaper column on 19 October 1945 and in the *Observer* newspaper on 10 March 1946. It appears Orwell was unaware that Swope had already created the phrase.

☆ FIRST country to constitutionally abolish its army

Costa Rica, Central America. Wednesday 1 December 1948

On this day, after victory in a civil war, Costa Rica's new President José Figueres Ferrer abolished the country's army and diverted the military budget into security, education and culture. In 1986, President Oscar Arias Sánchez declared 1 December the *Día de la Abolición del Ejército* – Military Abolition Day. Since the abolition, unlike its volatile neighbours, Costa Rica (literally 'Rich Coast') has not endured a civil war.

* LAST survivor of the Battle of Little Big Horn

Cavalry Private Charles A Windolph. Saturday 11 March 1950

At the Battle of the Little Big Horn Custer divided his men into three groups, Windolph being assigned to Company H under Colonel Frederick Benteen, who was ordered to explore a range of hills five miles from the village. Major Marcus Reno was to attack the Indian encampment from the upper end and Custer decided to strike further downstream. Reno soon discovered he was outnumbered and retreated to the river, where he was later joined by Benteen and his men. Custer continued his attack but was easily defeated by about 4,000 warriors, and all 264 of his men were killed. Meanwhile Reno and Benteen were also attacked and 47 men were killed before they were rescued by the arrival of General Alfred Terry and his army. During the fight Windolph showed such courage and resourcefulness that he was promoted sergeant on the battlefield. With co-author Robert Hunt he later wrote *I Fought with Custer: The Story of Sergeant Windolph, Last Survivor of the Battle of the Little Big Horn*. He died in Lead, South Dakota, on 11 March 1950 at the age of 98.

❑ ONLY cat to be awarded the Animal VC

Simon. Thursday 13 April 1950

In March 1948, seventeen-year-old Ordinary Seaman George Hickinbottom of British frigate HMS *Amethyst* found an ailing black and white cat wandering the dockyards of Hong Kong. He smuggled the cat aboard ship and nursed him back to health, after which 'Simon' became a favourite with the crew, who particularly appreciated his talent for killing the rats that infested the lower decks. Simon was soon adopted as the ship's cat and travelled with *Amethyst* up the Yangtze River to relieve HMS *Consort* in guarding the British Embassy at Nanking against communist insurgents. At 09:30 on 20 April 1949, about 100 miles upriver, the 'Yangtze Incident' began when communist shore batteries shelled the *Amethyst*. One shell tore through the captain's cabin, killing the captain and seriously wounding Simon, who vanished. *Amethyst* remained trapped and under attack for 101 days during which fifty shells hit home, killing seventeen crew members and wounding twenty-five. After a few days Simon reappeared, his whiskers and eyebrows singed off and his back and legs covered in dried blood. He was rushed to the medical bay, where four pieces of shrapnel were removed. In his absence the rats had overrun the ship but despite his wounds Simon returned to his former duties, killing at least one rat per day and raising the morale of sailors in the sick bay by sitting with them. On the night of 30 July 1949 acting commander Kerans made a daring run for freedom and, despite constant bombardment, made it to the open sea. The Yangtze Incident had been headline news but it was Simon who had captured people's hearts – waiting for him when the ship docked in Hong Kong were letters, poems and presents from all over the world, including tins of meat and cash for the crew to buy him extra cream. A 'cat officer' was appointed to deal with Simon's correspondence and it was decided to award him the Dickin Medal (the animal equivalent of the VC). *Amethyst* returned to England on 5 November 1949 and the medal ceremony was organised for 11 December in the presence of 79-year-old Marie Dickin, founder of the People's Dispensary for Sick Animals (PDSA), after whom the medal is named. Sadly, after catching a virus, and with a heart weakened by his war wounds, Simon died on 28 November before the presentation could be made. England went into mourning, a tribute appeared in the obituary columns of *The Times*, and hundreds of admirers, including the entire crew of HMS *Amethyst*, attended his funeral in the PDSA's animal cemetery in Ilford, East London. On 13 April 1950 Simon's Dickin Medal was accepted posthumously by Kerans. Simon's epitaph reads:

IN
MEMORY OF
'SIMON'
SERVED IN
H.M.S. AMETHYST
MAY 1948 – SEPTEMBER 1949
AWARDED DICKIN MEDAL
AUGUST 1949
DIED 28TH NOVEMBER 1949.
THROUGHOUT THE YANGTZE INCIDENT
HIS BEHAVIOUR WAS OF THE HIGHEST ORDER

☆ FIRST jet-to-jet aerial victory

Lockheed F80C v MiG-15. Korean War. Wednesday 8 November 1950

The first jet-to-jet aerial victory occurred when Lieutenant Russell John Brown Jr of the USAF 51st Fighter-Interceptor Wing, flying a Lockheed F-80C, shot down a Mikoyan Mig-15 of the People's Republic of China Air Force over Sinuiju on the Yalu River, which forms the border between North Korea and China.

❑ ONLY British general buried at Arlington Cemetery

Major General Orde Charles Wingate DSO, Arlington Cemetery, Virginia, USA. Friday 10 November 1950

Wingate was a brilliant and unorthodox military leader who helped to develop modern warfare through the creation of two special military units during the Second World War. He fought in three campaigns – Palestine, Ethiopia and Burma – rising in half a dozen years from Captain to Major General. Wingate's deep penetration counter-insurgency operations in pre-war British Palestine helped to lay the groundwork for the survival of the future nation of Israel. To achieve this he created the Special Night Squad in June 1938, shocking his political masters by drafting in members of Haganah, the illegal Jewish underground, to fight alongside soldiers of the Crown – the first instance of the British recognising Haganah's legitimacy as a Jewish defence force. Wingate became a hero of the Yishuv (the Jewish Community), and to this day is known in Israel as 'The Friend', his secret call sign during the Palestine campaign. In Ethiopia Wingate once achieved the surrender of 14,000 Italian troops by firing a single piece of captured artillery from different points to convince the enemy they were hopelessly surrounded, as a result of which his unorthodox Gideon Force (named after the biblical judge who defeated a large force with a tiny band) captured Addis Ababa. In Burma he pioneered modern mobile warfare techniques with his 'Chindits' (a corruption of the word for the mythical Burmese lion the 'Chinthe') – groups of daring British, Gurkha and Burmese guerrillas which harassed the numerically superior Japanese forces. He was the first military leader to link air power with ground forces, thus ensuring indefinite supplies for his guerrillas even behind enemy lines. As well as being a brilliant, innovative soldier Wingate was also highly eccentric, often wearing ill-fitting, grease-stained uniforms and an old-style pith helmet or appearing at meetings totally naked. In Palestine, recruits became used to him coming out of the shower to give them orders, wearing nothing but a shower cap, and continuing to scrub himself with a shower brush or a toothbrush. He ate little but grapes and raw onions, keeping one onion on a string around his neck for emergency snacks, and applied meat dripping to his scalp as a hair restorer. On 24 March 1944, the 41-year-old Wingate was returning to India from Burma when the US B-25 Mitchell plane in which he was flying crashed into a jungle-covered mountain, where he died alongside nine others. An expedition sent to find the wreckage discovered scattered unidentifiable remains, which were collected and buried on a mound with a bronze plate engraved with the names of all who perished in the plane. In April 1947 these remains were reburied at the British Military Cemetery at Imphal, India and finally, in November 1950, they were disinterred and taken to Arlington National Cemetery, Virginia. This was done because the remains of the different men could not be separated, and Allied rules stated that they must be repatriated and buried in the country of the majority of those who had died. The gravestone, which includes the name of the British army's 'favourite madman', is located at Section 12, No 288.

✱ LAST day of the First World War

Andorra, Pyrenees. Thursday 18 September 1958

The General Armistice of 11 November 1918 began the peace, and the Great War officially ended on 2 July 1921 with the peace conference at Versailles. That is, the war ended for everyone except the citizens of the tiny Pyreneean republic of Andorra, which declared war on Germany on 4 August 1914 but was not invited to sign the Treaty of Versailles. Presumably fed up with waiting, the Andorrans eventually enacted a decree on 18 September 1958 officially declaring that war had ended. This means Andorra was officially at war for forty-four years, one month and fourteen days.

❑ ONLY court martial for peeling potatoes improperly

Andrew God Jr, Fort Myer, Virginia, USA. June 1959

God – a 25-year-old architect before being drafted – was so bored of peeling potatoes that he began 'hacking the daylights out of the spuds', so his mess sergeant reported him for playing the fool. When God's commanding officer, Captain Thomas Woods, sentenced him to two hours' hard labour every day for fourteen days, God demanded a summary court-martial, as was his right under the 1951 Uniform Code of Military Justice. The charge was:

> having knowledge of a lawful order ... to peel and eye potatoes as directed, an order which it was his duty to obey, [he failed] to obey the same. [He] did, without proper authority, wilfully suffer potatoes, of some value, military property of the U.S., to be destroyed by improper peeling.

The mess sergeant testified that God had deliberately removed the eyes in thick wedges and sliced off random peels in flat slabs instead of removing them 'nice and thin'. Then, armed with a potato and peeler, the mess sergeant demonstrated God's technique by hacking away until the potato looked like a strand of spaghetti. For the defence, a mess sergeant from another company testified that God's peelings were quite normal considering he had only a knife to work with instead of a potato-peeler. Then, with cutting irony, the defence counsel proved that God's peelings (saved as evidence by the company commander) weighed less than those carved by his own mess sergeant. The case was dismissed and God got off scot-free. Why the charge was ever bought in the first place God only knows.

❏ ONLY Green Beret to achieve a No 1 record on the US Billboard chart

Staff Sergeant Barry Sadler, US Army Special Forces 'Green Beret'. Tuesday 15 March 1966

Sadler was an American author and musician who served as a Green Beret medic during the Vietnam War. In May 1965, while leading a patrol, he was severely wounded in the knee by a faeces-covered punji stick, which resulted in him being repatriated for major surgery. While he was recuperating a friend suggested he write a tribute song to his fellow Green Berets, so he wrote a twelve-verse lyric and submitted it to publisher Chet Gierlach, who showed it to Robin Moore, author of the book *The Green Beret* (later turned into a feature film starring John Wayne). Moore and Sadler rewrote the song, recorded it on 18 December 1965, and issued a special release for the military. But the song was so popular that Moore took it to RCA, who financed a full orchestral recording which was released on 11 January 1966, selling more than a million copies in a fortnight and becoming RCA's fastest-selling single of all time. On 5 March 1966 it knocked Nancy Sinatra's 'These Boots are Made for Walking' off the top spot. Although Sadler was a one-hit wonder so far as music was concerned, he enjoyed a successful second career as an author and created the 'Casca' series, relating the adventures of Casca Rufio Longinius, a Roman centurion who witnessed the crucifixion of Jesus, and who, for mocking him, was condemned to live through eternity as a mercenary. Sadler died on 5 November 1989, four days after his 49th birthday.

DID YOU KNOW?

Edson Raff, one of the first Special Forces officers, is credited with introducing the green beret, which was first given official recognition on President John F Kennedy's visit to the Special Warfare Center at Fort Bragg, North Carolina, on 12 October 1961. Kennedy instructed the Center's commander, Brigadier General William P Yarborough, that he wanted all Special Forces soldiers to wear the green beret, stating that because the Special Forces had a special mission they should have something exclusive that set them apart from the rest. Kennedy said that he regarded the Green Beret as 'a symbol of excellence, a badge of courage, a mark of distinction in the fight for freedom'.

☆ FIRST sinking of a large warship by a surface-to-surface guided missile

Eilat, *Mediterranean Sea. Monday 9 October 1967*

Two Egyptian power-boats sheltering in the entrance to Alexandria Harbour fired Russian Styx missiles at the Israeli destroyer *Eilat*. The Israeli battleship was on a routine watch 25 miles away when the missiles struck and sank it, killing 47 crew members.

❏ **ONLY** US naval ship to surrender in peacetime without a fight

USS Pueblo, *North Korean waters. Tuesday 23 January 1968*

On 23 January 1968 USS *Pueblo*, a highly sophisticated electronic intelligence-gathering ship, was surrounded by three 50-knot torpedo boats and two submarine chasers after allegedly straying into North Korean territorial waters – although US Naval authorities and the crew of the *Pueblo* insist that the US ship was several miles outside North Korean waters. One of the North Korean submarine chasers began firing 57mm cannons, killing US fireman Duane D Hodges and wounding several of the crew including *Pueblo*'s Commander Lloyd Mark Bucher. Bucher surrendered and the Koreans boarded his ship and took it to Wonsan, North Korea, after tying up crew members, blindfolding them and prodding them with bayonets. Bucher and his crew were interned in a prisoner of war camp where they claim they were starved and regularly tortured – and things got worse after the North Koreans learned that crewmen were giving them 'the finger' in staged propaganda photos. Bucher and the surviving 82 crew members were eventually released after a written admission by the USA that USS *Pueblo* had been spying, together with an apology and an assurance that the US would not spy in the future. On 23 December 1968, exactly eleven months after being taken prisoner, the crew was taken to the border with South Korea and ordered to walk south across the 'Bridge of No Return' – at which the US immediately retracted all 'confessions'. The *Pueblo* remains a commissioned vessel of the US Navy but is still held by the North Koreans, providing one of the main tourist attractions in Pyongyang, having attracted over 250,000 visitors since being put on display.

✳ LAST grog ration

Royal Navy. Thursday 30 July 1970

Grog was an official alcoholic drink issued to sailors serving aboard Her Majesty's ships, comprising rum diluted with water. This dilution was named after Admiral Edward Vernon, who introduced it into the Royal Navy on 21 January 1740 to reduce the drunkenness caused by neat rum – his nickname was 'Old Grog', after the large cloak he always wore made of a coarse fabric called 'grogram'. (This delightful story is suspect, since the word 'grog' appears in a book written by Daniel Defoe in 1718, 22 years before Vernon's order to dilute the rum ration). The daily ration was originally one pint of rum, issued twice daily in half-pint measures. The issue involved an elaborate ritual which began at 11:00 when the boatswain's mate piped 'Up spirits', the signal for the petty officer of the day to climb to the quarterdeck and collect the keys to the spirit room from an officer. Then the ship's cooper and a detachment of Royal Marines would unlock the door of the spirit room and witness the pumping into a keg of rum rations for every rating and petty officer on the ship aged twenty or more and not under punishment. Two marines would then lift the keg to the deck, standing guard while a file of cooks from the petty officers' messes held out their jugs and the sergeant of marines ladled out the authorised number of 'tots' (half-pints). The rest of the rum was mixed in a tub with two parts water, becoming the grog provided to the ratings. At noon the boatswain's mate piped 'Muster for rum'. The petty officers were served first, and entitled to take their rum undiluted, while the ratings drank their grog in one long gulp when they finished their work around noon – teetotal sailors could receive cash instead of alcohol. The practice of serving grog twice a day was also adopted by both the Continental Navy (the forerunner of the US Navy, *see 1775*) and the US Navy, and Robert Smith, then Secretary of the US Navy, experimented with substituting native rye whiskey for rum – American sailors preferred it, the change was made permanent, and it became known in the US Navy as 'Bob Smith' instead of grog. The last US Navy grog ration was served on 31 August 1862 before the practice was abolished on 1 September. Meanwhile, in 1850, the British Navy ration was reduced to one gill of rum diluted, with extra rum rations provided for special celebrations such as Trafalgar Day. The Royal Navy grog ration was finally outlawed by the Admiralty in 1970, and the last piping of 'Up Spirits' was heard on 30 July, known ever since as 'Black Tot Day'.

DID YOU KNOW?

Admiral Vernon, after whom grog is named, also gave his name to the home of George Washington, whose brother named it Mount Vernon in honour of the British admiral.

* LAST US soldier killed in combat in the Vietnam War

Lieutenant Colonel William Benedict Nolde, US Army, An Loc, Vietnam. Saturday 27 January 1973

Before joining the army Nolde was a professor of military science at Central Michigan University. As a US Army officer he served in both the Korean War and the Vietnam War, accumulating four medals including the Bronze Star and Legion of Merit. On 27 January 1973 the 43-year-old father of five was killed by an artillery shell just eleven hours before the US signed the Paris Peace Accords. He was the 45,941[st] and last American soldier listed as having been killed in combat in Vietnam since 1961, and whilst other Americans were killed after the truce was enacted, these were not recorded as combat casualties. Nolde was given a full military funeral at Arlington National Cemetery on 5 February1973, at which his coffin was accompanied by the same riderless horse that had accompanied the coffin at President Kennedy's funeral (*see Last US Army horse, below*).

DID YOU KNOW?

USAF pilot First Lieutenant Michael Joseph Blassie was also killed near An Loc when his A-37B went down on 11 May 1972. From 1984 to 1988 he was buried in the Tomb of the Unknowns as the Unknown Service Member from the Vietnam War, before positive identification was obtained. (*See 11 November 1920*)

✻ LAST US Army horse

Black Jack. Friday 6 February 1976

Black Jack was born on 19 January 1947, and on 22 November 1953 he was sent from Fort Reno, Oklahoma, to the Third Infantry ('The Old Guard') at Fort Myer, Virginia. Named after General John J 'Black Jack' Pershing, Supreme Commander of the American Expeditionary Force in the First World War, he served in numerous ceremonial functions including the funerals of Presidents Herbert Hoover, John F Kennedy, Lyndon B Johnson and General Douglas MacArthur. Riderless, and attentively following the flag-draped coffin with the empty, reversed boots shining in the stirrups, Black Jack became a symbol of national loss, performing the same duty for hundreds of other funeral processions at Arlington National Cemetery. He was the last horse issued to the US Army by the Quartermaster and the last to carry the 'US' brand with which all army horses were marked. He was semi-retired on 1 June 1973, and died on 6 February 1976, at the age of 29. His ashes lie in an urn at his monument at Fort Meyer.

* LAST military invasion of British sovereign soil
* LAST battle on British sovereign soil

Invasion of the Falkland Islands and the Battle for Port Stanley.
Falklands War. Friday 2 April 1982 and Monday 14 June 1982.

On 19 March 1982 a group of Argentinian scrap merchants
landed on the uninhabited British Crown Colony of South
Georgia, in the South Atlantic, and raised the Argentinian flag.
This may have seemed like a harmless prank, except that
Argentina had long disputed British ownership of South Georgia
and the neighbouring Falkland Islands, and Argentinian president
General Leopoldo Galtieri was looking for a distraction from
domestic political problems – two weeks later, on 2 April, Galtieri
followed the scrap merchants' lead by launching a full military
invasion of *Las Malvinas*, as the Falklands are known in
Argentina. Within three hours the Argentinian forces had
overwhelmed the seventy Royal Marines garrisoned on the islands
in what British Foreign Secretary Lord Carrington described as a
'great national humiliation'. Prime Minister Margaret Thatcher
immediately resolved to retake the islands, assembling a task force
of more than seventy ships which arrived in Falklands waters on
22 April. Three days later the Royal Marines retook South Georgia
and on 1 May British planes began bombing the airfield at Port
Stanley, the capital of the Falklands. But the war did not begin in
earnest until 2 May, when the British submarine HMS *Conqueror*
controversially sank the Argentinian cruiser *General Belgrano*,
killing 368 Argentine sailors. Two days later the Argentinians
responded by sinking the British destroyer HMS *Sheffield* (the
first major British warship to be sunk since the Second World
War) despite which the task force succeeded in landing troops and
launching a ground assault. The main British counter-invasion
began on 21 May when some 5,000 troops went ashore at

San Carlos Bay on East Falkland, and during the next week British forces recaptured key settlements before linking up with reinforcements who had been landed at Bluff Cove for the final assault on Port Stanley. This last battle lasted from 11 to 14 June and entailed breaking a ring of Argentine defences in six separate engagements at Mount Longdon, Two Sisters, Mount Harriet, Tumbledown Mountain, Wireless Ridge and Mount William. Argentine resistance was eventually broken and the invaders began retreating into Port Stanley itself, where, according to one press report, 'white flags began to blossom like flowers' and the Argentinians capitulated without further action. At a cost of 255 British and 652 Argentinian lives the Falklands were back in British hands, and in London Thatcher told parliament that victory had been 'boldly planned, bravely executed and brilliantly accomplished'. Throughout the campaign government spin doctors insisted on referring to the war euphemistically as the 'Falklands Conflict', as recorded by Sue Townsend in her comic novel *The Diary of Adrian Mole, aged 13 3/4*, in which the eponymous Adrian Mole notes: 'The nation has been told that we are not at war, we are at conflict.'

❏ ONLY war to last more than three centuries

Scilly-Dutch War. Thursday 17 April 1986

During the seventeenth century the Dutch navy suffered heavy losses from the British Royalist fleet based in Scilly. On 30 March 1651, Dutch Admiral Maarten Harpertszoon Tromp arrived in the Scilly Isles with twelve men-of-war to secure reparation and to put an end to the plundering of Dutch merchant ships by pirates based in the Scillies. Tromp demanded the surrender of the islanders, who were the last Royalists holding out at the end of the English Civil War. The islanders refused and Tromp declared war but before the situation could escalate British Admiral Robert Blake arrived with the English Parliamentary Fleet. Blake promised that he could resolve the situation without Dutch intervention and Tromp, satisfied, sailed away – but because the incident had ended peacefully everyone forgot that Tromp had not withdrawn his declaration of war. In September 1985 Scilly councillors realised that hostilities had never officially ended, and the Dutch Ministry confirmed that a state of war was still in force. The following April, Dutch Ambassador Jonkheer Rein Huydecoper flew to the Scillies to deliver the official proclamation that hostilities were over. Thus ended the 335 year war in which no shots were fired and no blood was shed – probably the Scillyest war of all time.

✳ LAST surviving VC-winner of the First World War

Captain Ferdinand Maurice Felix 'Freddie' West (later Air Commodore). Friday 8 July 1988

West was an eighteen-year-old bank clerk when the First World War began. After enlisting in the Fusiliers he became convinced that 'trench warfare was for rats not men' and instead joined the Royal Flying Corps. On 10 August 1918 he spotted a huge concentration of German troops and transport near Roye, France, and in an attempt to get accurate figures of the enemy's strength he repeatedly flew through a hail of machine-gun fire. He was then attacked by German scouts, one of whose bullets smashed through the cockpit, severely wounding his right foot, but despite the pain he dived into cloud cover and re-emerged to make further observations. Turning for home he was attacked by several more scouts and took five shots in his left leg which smashed the bone and severed an artery. Still under fire, West managed to twist the leg of his khaki shorts into a makeshift tourniquet, fly to safety and then, facing collapse from loss of blood, make a desperate but safe landing on rough ground whereupon some Canadian troops rushed to his aid. He forced himself to stay conscious until he was able to make a full report to a senior officer, then promptly fainted. He lost his left leg but won the VC. Although invalided out of active service West was soon back as the RAF's first diplomat at the Foreign Office where, incredibly, both his army and navy counterparts also had wooden legs. A little later he became Douglas Bader's commanding officer when Bader lost both his legs. West died on 8 July 1988 at the age of 92, the last of the First World War VC-winners to pass on.

DID YOU KNOW?

West was fitted with an artificial leg in Roehampton, England, but with his £250 compensation he went to Paris where he paid for a superior wooden leg and later an even better one made by the Swiss tool manufacturer de Soutter, who had also lost a leg.

❏ ONLY surrender induced by rock 'n' roll

Manuel Noriega, Panama, Operation Just Cause. Wednesday 3 January 1990

On 20 December 1989 US President George H W Bush launched Operation Just Cause, an invasion of Panama by 25,000 US personnel to remove dictator Juan Manuel Noriega. Noriega fled the attack and a manhunt finally tracked him down to the Apostolic Nunciature, the Holy See's embassy in Panama, where he had taken refuge. US troops established a perimeter around the building which, as an embassy, was considered sovereign soil of the Vatican and could not be taken directly as this would constitute an invasion of Vatican City. However, troops guarding it developed a cunning plan to use psychological warfare. Knowing Noriega's passion for opera they attempted to force him out by blasting a barrage of non-stop hard rock music outside the residence. Many of the records were specifically chosen for their titles, for example, 'Dead Man's Party', 'The Party's Over' and 'Judgement Day'; reportedly Van Halen's 'Panama' was also played repeatedly. The Vatican, wanting harmony, complained to President Bush and US troops stopped the noise. However, Noriega surrendered to US Forces on 3 January 1990, after which he was flown to Miami and in April 1992 tried on eight counts of drug trafficking, racketeering, and money laundering. He was found guilty and sentenced to forty years in prison, reduced in 1999 to thirty years.

DID YOU KNOW?

The complete Noriega playlist can be read on George Washington University's National Security Archive website. Selected highlights include: '(You've Got) Another Thing Coming' – Judas Priest; 'Danger Zone' – Kenny Loggins; 'Dead Man's Party' – Oingo Boingo; 'Don't Look Back' – Boston; 'Electric Spanking of War Babies' – Funkadelic; 'Heaven's On Fire' – Kiss; 'If I Had A Rocket Launcher' – Bruce Cockburn; 'In My Time of Dying' – Led Zeppelin; 'Iron Man' – Black Sabbath; 'Judgement Day' – Whitesnake; 'Jungle Love' – Steve Miller; 'No More Mister Nice Guy' – Alice Cooper; 'Paradise City' – Guns N' Roses; 'Panama' – Van Halen; 'Paranoid' – Black Sabbath; 'Refugee' – Tom Petty; 'Renegade' – Styx; 'Run Like Hell' – Pink Floyd; 'The Party's Over' – Journey; 'This Means War' – Joan Jett; 'Wanted Dead or Alive' – Bon Jovi; 'Wanted Man' – Ratt; 'War Pigs' – Black Sabbath; 'We're Not Gonna Take It' – Twisted Sister; 'You Shook Me All Night Long' – AC/DC; 'Your Time is Gonna Come' – Led Zeppelin.

❏ ONLY war predicted by pizzas

Operation Desert Storm. Gulf War. 05:00 Wednesday 16 January 1991

In January 1991 the whole of the US was aware that war with Iran was likely and imminent, but nobody knew for certain if or when it would happen. On the night of 15/16 January the Domino's Pizza franchise near the Pentagon received hundreds of orders for pizza from the Defense Department. It became increasingly obvious that something major was afoot and at 05:00 on 16 January, Domino's issued a warning to all its franchisees that war was likely to begin later that day. They were proved right when a US-led United Nations coalition launched Operation Desert Storm and began the Gulf War.

✳ LAST survivor of the Boer War

George Frederick Ives. Monday 12 April 1993

Born in France on 17 November 1881 the son of a coachman and a lady's maid, Ives was taken to England as an infant to avoid being conscripted in the French army as he grew up. Ironically, he was one of the 123 volunteers to join the 1st Imperial Yeomanry at Cheltenham, of whom only seventeen survived the Boer War. As a mounted infantryman, his job was to chase enemy commandos but he had little enthusiasm for the British cause and a deep sympathy for the Boers fighting for their own country. Nevertheless, he said that, as a soldier, 'My job was to get over there and kill Boers, you went to war to kill someone and they tried to kill you back.' After the war – in which he was permanently scarred by a Boer bullet that ricocheted off a rock and grazed his neck – he emigrated to Canada and became a farmer. He married his wife Kay in 1910 – a marriage that would last until her death 76 years later – and worked as a farmer until retiring at sixty, after which he spent fifteen years working in a shipyard. He remained remarkably fit and could do full chin-ups to a parallel bar until well over the age of 100. He died on 12 April 1993 in Aldergrove, British Columbia, at the age of 111.

✻ LAST survivor of the ANZACs who landed on the first day at Gallipoli

Corporal Ted Matthews. Tuesday 9 December 1997

Eighteen-year-old Sydney carpenter Ted Matthews was among the very first ANZAC (Australian and New Zealand Army Corps) troops to go ashore with the 1st Division Signals on 25 April 1915, the first day of the disastrous invasion of Gallipoli. The first 15,000 troops were dropped at the wrong beach, with no cover from the Turkish guns firing down from the steep cliffs above, and as Matthews splashed in the water heading for the beach he was struck by shrapnel and only saved by a pocket-book given to him by his mother. He had been at Gallipoli for almost eight months when he and his comrades were evacuated in the single most successful action of the campaign, in which not one soldier was killed. In the entire time he was there Mathews fired only two shots at the Turks – both at the same man. He later said, 'And I hope I missed the poor bugger.' He died in Sydney on 9 December 1997 at the age of 101.

DEDICATIONS & ACKNOWLEDGEMENTS

For Ann & Norman Lawrence for being beacons of thoughtfulness and generosity.

Jeremy and Ian would like to thank:

Sue Beadle
Malcolm Croft
Paul Donnelly
Roddy Langley
Norman Lawrence
Linda Yaffe
Household Cavalry Regimental Museum
Imperial War Museum
RAF Museum

Jeremy Beadle is nationally known for a series of hugely successful TV 'people' shows. But for years he has quietly hunted the odd curious and maverick side of life. He is lucky to have missed conscription so his military experience is limited. However; the Royal Navy once lent him a destroyer and frigate; he survived the Commando assault course with the Marines at Lympstone, Devon ; entertained the Army in Kosovo and the RAF in the Falklands; spent six weeks locked in the dungeons of the 19th Century Spit Bank Fort in the Solent; and was part of the largest airborne invasion of France since World War Two (a mass-balloon crossing of the English Channel in aid of Children with Leukaemia).

Ian Harrison has written more than twenty books on subjects ranging from ancient battlefields to modern airports. His titles include *Where Were You When. . . ?* (Collins & Brown/Anova) and the popular *Book of Firsts* and *Book of Lasts*, which between them have been translated in to sixteen languages. Ian's military career peaked at 17 when he was promoted Chief Cadet Captain of the Nautical College, Pangbourne; like Jeremy, he has survived the Royal Marines assault course at Lympstone.